Atisa and the Time Machine
In Search of
Kalidasa

Atisa and the Time Machine
In Search of
Kalidasa

Anu Kumar

JAICO PUBLISHING HOUSE

Ahmedabad Bangalore Bhopal Bhubaneswar Chennai
Delhi Hyderabad Kolkata Lucknow Mumbai

Published by Jaico Publishing House
A-2 Jash Chambers, 7-A Sir Phirozshah Mehta Road
Fort, Mumbai - 400 001
jaicopub@jaicobooks.com
www.jaicobooks.com

ATISA AND THE TIME MACHINE
IN SEARCH OF KALIDASA
ISBN 978-81-8495-629-0

First Jaico Impression: 2014

Printed by

For Ajay, Devyani and of course all my readers

Contents

Acknowledgments

Vatsala Kaul Banerjee, then at Puffin, loved the idea of Atisa – *Atisa and the Seven Wonders* could come to life only with her. I'd like to thank Sudeshna Shome Ghosh too, also at Puffin, for her wonderful support and encouragement. My parents, Chinmay and Uma Chakrabarty and my siblings Dhruba and Soma, who have always been very supportive.

Kanishka Gupta of Writers' Side helped in getting me in touch with Jaico. And to Akash Shah, publisher and my editors Sandhya Iyer and Srija Basu, to whom I am deeply grateful for their faith in the idea, their love of the concept and for all their encouragement to this book and the series. Priya Kuriyan's wonderful illustrations have rendered that special touch. Most importantly, I am thankful to all my readers who have loved Atisa and wanted him back. The past stretches a long way back and some adventures have only just begun.

Preface

Atisa and his Time Machine: In search of Kalidasa is the third of Atisa's adventures into the past and a different time period. For those of you reading this first, and I hope you will read the other two books too, a little preliminary explanation is always useful.

Atisa lives with his parents in Tawang, far in the northeast of India. His father, who is the inventor and scientist Gesar runs a flying school there, while Gaea named after the ancient Greek Earth goddess, is his archaeologist explorer mother. Atisa's teacher who is affectionately called Elder Lama lives at the monastery next door when he is not travelling. It is from Elder Lama that Atisa learns the ancient languages, Prakrit, the more difficult Sanskrit, and he even possesses a smattering of Latin and Aramaic - a knowledge that has often helped him in his adventures.

It is Atisa's flying machine that helps him bridge the time divide. This flying machine came his way right at the very beginning of *Atisa and the Seven Wonders*. It was designed by the ancient Greek inventor, famous in myth, called Daedelus. The latter grateful for Atisa's help in finding his lost son, Icarus, presents the machine to him. Later, Atisa's inventor father, Gesar makes several additions to it. These include the amazing sound catcher that can catch voices and sounds across millions of miles - sounds that belong to another age, and those that are missed by even the most advanced machines of the world.

The next book in the series, *Adventures with Hieun Tsang* has Atisa travelling in the footsteps of the Chinese monk Hieun Tsang in the early seventh century CE. Now Gesar has added a special lantern to his flying machine and its light changes colour with the weather. In this, the third adventure, *In Search of Kalidasa*, Gesar has finally perfected the language decoder, that he has been working on for some time.

In the following adventures, Gesar plans to add more to the flying machine, though he and Gaea worry constantly every time Atisa moves back into the past. Atisa believes that knowing the past helps in better understanding the present and the future!

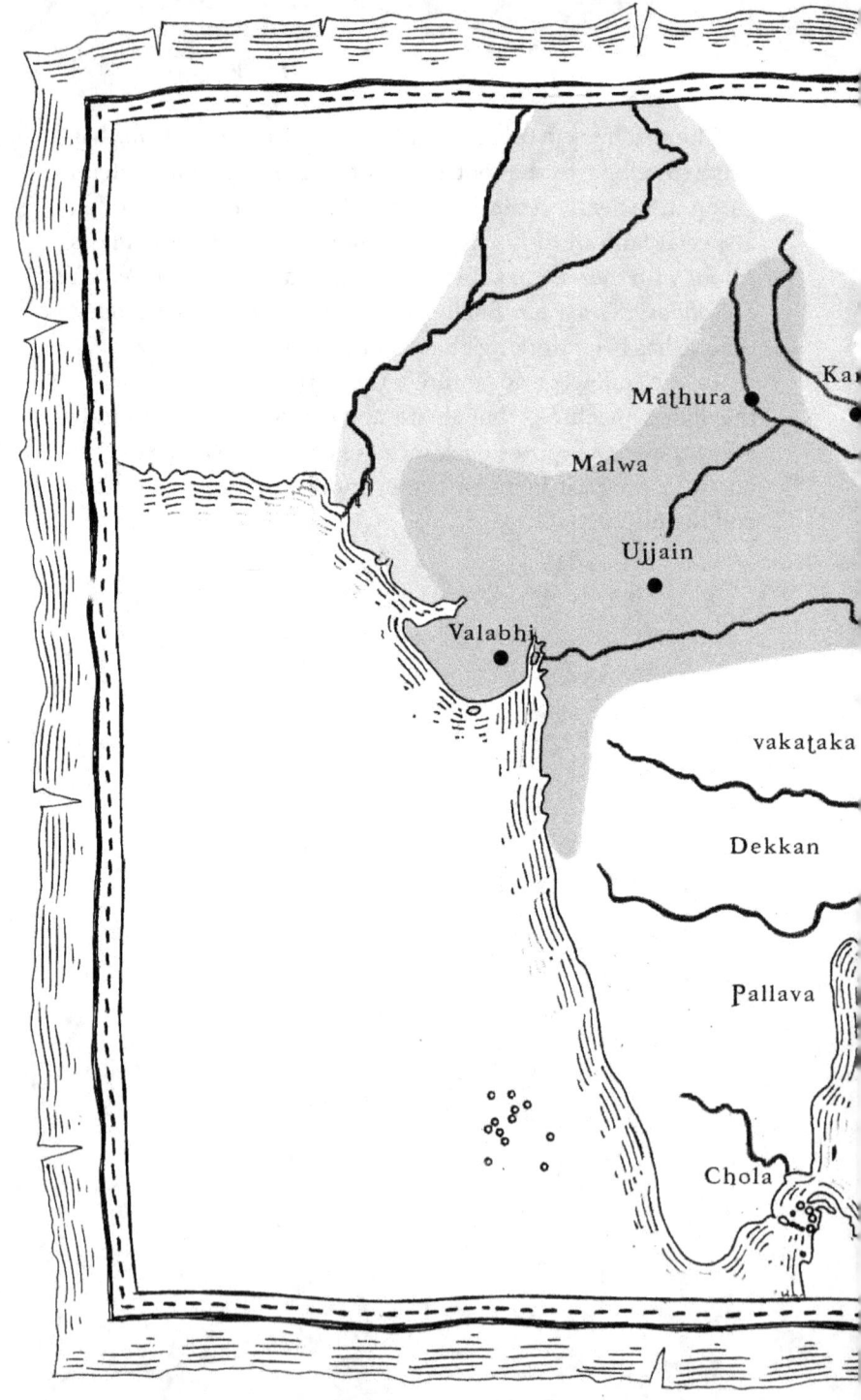

Ka

Mathura

Malwa

Ujjain

Valabhi

vakaṭaka

Dekkan

Pallava

Chola

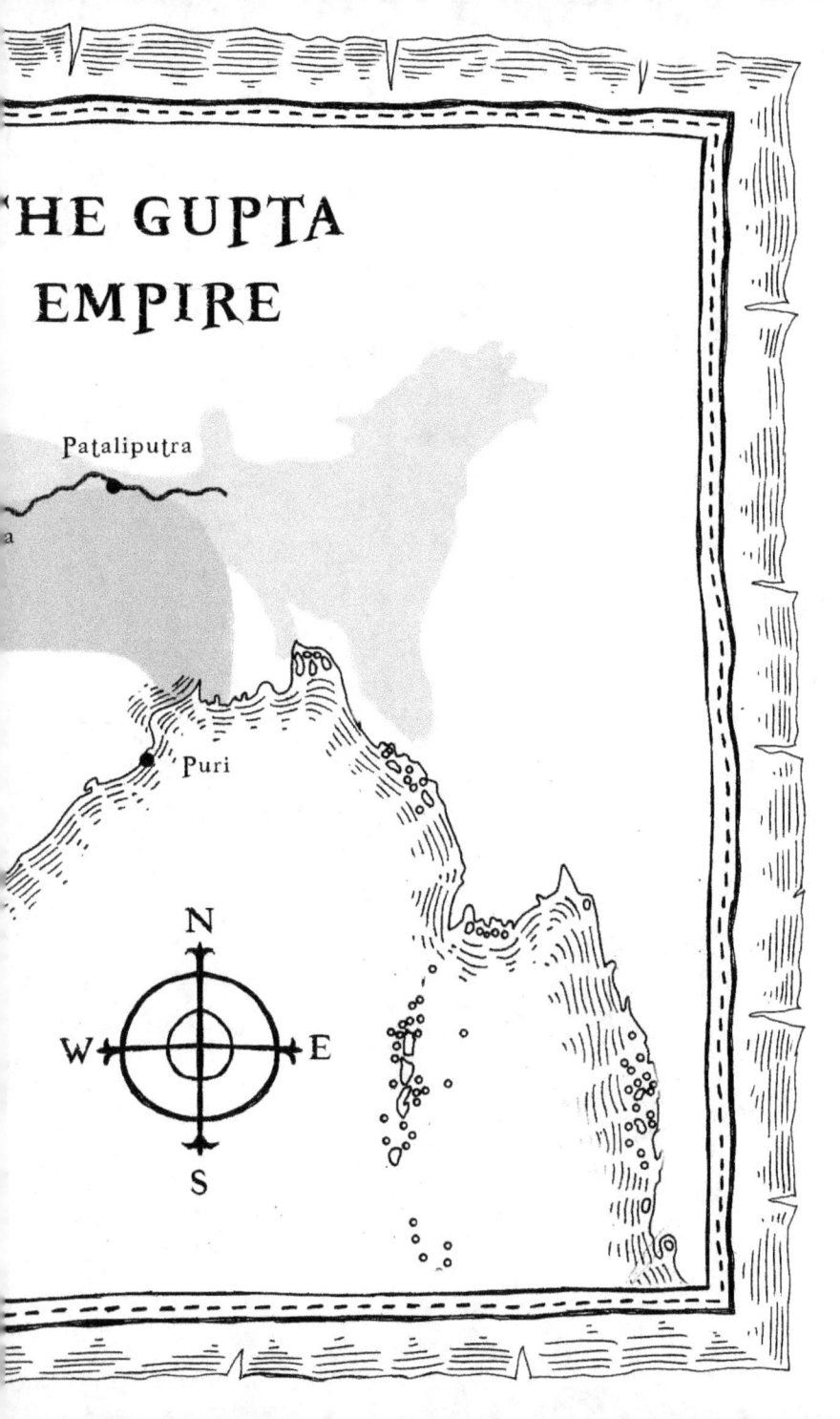

Prologue
Home Again

That year winter had come late to the mountains, but it seemed everyone already had somewhere to be. Many though were travelling just to catch the eclipse, one of the rarest to occur ever. The Moon, the planet Mars and the Earth would be aligned with each other, in one perfect line, facing the majestic sun. And the earth's shadow would blank out the moon, with Mars appearing far away, as a cold unblinking red dot in a dark universe. Atisa, however, was at home, still making his plans. Home was right next to the monastery at Tawang in the eastern Himalayas, where Atisa lived with his parents, who were often away travelling – his scientist father Gesar and his archaeologist mother Gaea. That winter Atisa would soon leave to join his mother on her latest expedition. Gaea was on a new mission to retrace the secret routes of a tribe called the Sakas, who centuries ago, had travelled across India, moving from the mountains of the north-west, all the way to central India.

Atisa was presently engrossed with the strange, exciting emails he had exchanged a while ago with his teacher, Elder Lama. The emails were to do with his father's latest mission. It was as exciting an adventure as the one Gaea had set out on. Gesar was headed with his team towards Mount Everest, and they would attempt the world's first skydiving mission over the world's highest peak. The team carried some very advanced equipment including special effect cameras, some of which Gesar had designed himself, to photograph the eclipse.

It was a mission deemed almost impossible, but his father and his team had been training hard for it. 'It is important we do this,' Gesar had told him. 'There is the most unusual eclipse of the moon expected, a rare event. Mars, the Moon and the Earth will fall in a straight line for a few moments.' Elder Lama's emails on the same subject had been even more interesting. According to him, an eclipse such as this one had last occurred more than 1800 years ago. He had dug this story out from old texts in the library of the Tawang monastery. 'There is indeed an old manuscript that tells of this eclipse,' he had written. 'But we only have half of it. Perhaps the rest of it is lying around, forgotten and obscure, in some old library. The ancient astronomer Varahamihira is believed to have composed it. But the thing is, Varahamihira is supposed to have lived at a later time, a little after the time of the eclipse.' Atisa could well imagine the rueful look on Elder Lama's face as he ended his email. Elder Lama travelled often, teaching theology in several universities, and could be very mysterious on email. In the end, it was Atisa's mother who explained the confusion over Varahamihira. 'Stories have it that Varahamihira lived in King Chandragupta Vikramaditya's time, which was almost 1800 years ago.'

'He was one of the Nine Gems in the king's court,' she went on. 'But historical accounts place him a hundred years later. It could also be that he came from a family of astronomers, many of whom had the same name. Indeed, the Varahamihira who wrote this book might have lived several decades after the one who lived in the king's court.' She had ended with a twinkle in her eye, knowing Atisa was all confused and intrigued. All Elder Lama had let on in his last email was this:

Wait till I find out more. Let me have my own adventure. In the meantime, maybe you can do a little research for me. Atisa groaned as he read it. Elder Lama's research usually had him poring over old texts. But as he read on, he was surprised at being proved wrong. *When you are on the way to join your mother's expedition, you will come to a small town called Jhansi.* Jhansi... Atisa stopped in surprise. It was a place his mother had mentioned too. *It is older than you think. The ancient astronomer Varahamihira lived there. He came from a renowned family of astronomers who experimented and wrote a great many books. They lived in Jhansi, and perhaps you may have things to find out there. How did the text on the eclipse get lost, and what happened to the other half? Will you try?*

'Yes,' he had mouthed the answer to himself, 'it does sound exciting.'

The Voice from the Past

The sentry high at the tower post saw the advancing cloud of dust and knew it was time to make the announcement. Looking down, he saw a city buzzing in anticipation. Bells tolled in the light breeze, women waited holding plates of flowers up and clay lamps dozed along terraces and on porches. Even the boats anchored by the Ganga turned and swayed in the breeze; every creak held the sound of hope. The lamps would be lit once the emperor's army had been sighted.

The sentry lifted his trumpet, and its sound unfurled and swept over the city of Pataliputra, the capital of the kingdom of Magadha, which was now vaster than before, stretching from the Arabian Sea to its west to the east, close to the river Brahmaputra. It also became the seat of power from where Chandragupta Vikramaditya ruled over his empire, an empire that was now going to be massive. At sundown, the advance messenger from the far west had reached Pataliputra with the glad news: the Sakas had finally been defeated and emperor Vikramaditya had led his armies from the front. For decades, the empire's western frontier had remained unsettled, thanks to the many raids and invasions by the Sakas from the desert region of the north-west, and there was a real possibility of peace now.

The trumpet rang out again, and barely had its sounds died away when the sounds of cheering filled the city. The drummers thumped in joy, the sounds of ululation followed in joyous unison, and people on the streets stopped whatever they were doing and danced with abandon.

Varahamihira stood looking down from his chamber adjacent to the palace complex and ran thoughtful fingers down his beard. He was the emperor's trusted astronomer, known for his unique abilities to foretell the future, and there was a sombre look on his face. It lit up for a moment, when Lilavati, his daughter, came running up. 'It's too early to celebrate,' he said without turning around, 'but I am afraid I may sound like an old fogey if I am too cautious.'

She came up to him and touched his hand lightly in assurance. Varahamihira stood tall, and his beard almost reached his chest. But his usually intent eyes were now distracted and held worry. Lilavati knew what her father meant. The king's victory had come at a great cost. He had waged a long campaign that had kept him away from Pataliputra for more than a year, and then just before he had set off, there had come the news that his son-in-law, the brave king Rudrasena who ruled in the western regions, had been killed by the Sakas. Everyone grieved for Rudrasena's wife, Prabhavati, who was also Vikramaditya's daughter, even as they admired her, for she had stepped in to rule in his place and had proved herself worthy of her father. 'I am worried that the celebrations are a facade to distract the king and to get his attention away from things that matter,' said Varahamihira. Lilavati nodded. Below, they saw one of the courtiers, Dipanna, stand up on a podium and wave to the crowd. Looking up, his eyes darkened as he caught sight of father and daughter watching him. But as the cheering continued, he bowed mockingly towards them and unfurled the scroll he had in his hand.

'Let me read out a poem I have composed in the king's honour.' He looked around as a silence fell and added, 'No wonder, even the poet Kalidasa is not here. He is afraid his

brilliance will now be truly eclipsed.' Varahamihira turned away in disgust, and Lilavati, who was more discreet, turned away a moment or two later. As Dipanna's nasal voice filled the square below, she was convinced that even his best verses could not measure up to Kalidasa's most easily wrought compositions. Kalidasa, she thought, swinging her plaits back over her head, would always be the best. 'He will stop at nothing,' her father said, reading her thoughts. 'Dipanna hates Kalidasa, and his ambition far exceeds any talent he could ever have. These celebrations are all part of his plan, but it is too early, too grandiose. I fear the danger is not yet over.'

Lilavati looked up in alarm, as she saw her father scanning the skies anxiously. His seriousness in the midst of the cheer all around struck a chill in her heart, and her father never said such a thing lightly. 'There is something strange up in the skies,' her father shuddered, and it was not in fear but with barely concealed excitement that he continued, 'something we will be privy to, an event so rare that it could mean a lot of things. And it could be used by evil men for evil means.'

Lilavati too gasped with excitement. She knew her father was referring to the eclipse, a celestial event whose details her father had shared only with her. 'The eclipse has nothing to do with the future I see,' he said, 'and it will be difficult to convince many about this. But I see dangers ahead and the possibility of evil.'

He looked at his daughter and said no more. He couldn't bring himself to pass on his worries to her and wished there was someone who could stave off the dangers he foresaw. Varahamihira sighed and then smiled as he saw Lilavati's anxious face. He was wishing for a superman, someone with superhuman powers, a figure who could fly, run faster than a horse and do other wonderful things. He knew that it was too much to ask for. He shook his head and smiled. Someone even with a flying machine would be a big help.

'But won't you come down to join the fun, even for a few hours?' asked his daughter.

Her petulance made him relent and he said, 'You go ahead. I will clear my scrolls and be with you soon.'

Atisa was a few hundred miles away to the east and a thousand and more years apart from all this. He was still thinking of that email and about Varahamihira as he started his flying machine, which he had to test before he took off on a long journey anywhere. Elder Lama had left behind scattered pieces of a puzzle... an astronomer who lived a long time ago, right in Jhansi, almost in the heart of India, and a book on the eclipse, with half of its parts missing. Atisa's thoughts were as scattered, but just then he heard the first crackles on his sound catcher. It was a machine designed by Gesar to pick up voices from the past and every other sound that even the world's most advanced machines could miss. To Atisa, the crackles sounded like someone crunching up fistfuls of paper, and this was followed by the familiar bubble of static and popping balloon sounds that were always heard when the sound catcher had zoomed in on something. These sounds also reminded Atisa of the emptiness of space.

Atisa leant forward, his heart beating fast. He knew for sure his sound catcher had picked up something distinct. He could hear the wind race into the balloon's folds, as he bent and raised the volume of the sound catcher. There was again a bubble and a clatter, then a bit later a voice broke through, speaking excitedly. It was in a language he did not understand, and something about the voice, the way it broke and the deep intonations that marked every sentence, and his own intuition, told Atisa for sure that he was hearing a voice from the past.

He felt a familiar rush of excitement. The wind pulled his hair back and made the hair on his arm stand up. Barely had the voice faded when he felt the wind rush at him and his machine. The wind thundered, drumming inside the balloon's folds, and he held on fast as his cabin turned over again and again several times. He heard the voice and the crackles again, while the wind continued to blow. His machine bounced, swayed, whirled past clouds and turned over, but he held on fast, watching his breath mingle with fog as the cold clouds struck him on the face, and he tasted the mist on his lips time and again.

It took a long time for the storm to quieten, and the machine bobbed a few times before it settled down to an even pace. By then, as Atisa quelled his racing heart, it was late afternoon, the sound catcher was quiet and he knew he was several miles from home. Looking down, he saw that he was over the low brown mountains and the plateau of old granite that marked central India. He had been blown several hundred miles off course.

Now as he turned up the sound catcher, he heard the drumming of falling rocks, the pattering of waterfalls, bird calls and also the distant shouts of trekkers and helicopters. Then there was that voice again, clearer than ever before, breathless and still as excited, and he knew it was the same voice he had heard before. But this time, he sensed the terrible urgency in it as well, an urgency all the more apparent because of the quiet that stretched for long moments. Nothing else sounded on the sound catcher, after the first words spoken in a rushed, nervous, yet considered manner. It was as if the speaker had rehearsed, even in his panic. And so Atisa waited. The hills below looked serenely old and very captivating. He looked again at his sound catcher, and then as if he had willed it to speak up, the light on the machine flashed and he heard the voice again.

The voice still sounded frantic, and it was clear that the man was very afraid, that he was repeating his words too. Atisa could almost see him, looking over his shoulder as he spoke. It was a desperate call for help.

Later, as the silence settled in quickly, Atisa copied the message as best as he remembered it. He had written it down just as he thought it sounded, words that he knew belonged to another language. But he couldn't copy the clear panic and despair the voice carried.

He pushed the paper into his pocket and shivered, as the cold wind pushed against his neck and the gooseflesh rose like small thorns on his arms. It was the strangest message he had ever received, in the strangest manner possible. He didn't want to give in to his doubts just yet, but on an impulse, he moved his machine low and lower still, hoping to trace the voice to where the signals had been strongest. He was afraid the rocks would graze his flying machine, but the land gave nothing away, and this time the voice had well and truly vanished.

A while later, he thought he heard a splutter again, but no words burst through the sound catcher. This time he was sailing over the ravines, and looking down, he saw the deep gash on the earth, plunging down till brown turned absolutely dark. And he saw nothing, except in the thin stretch of a river not too far away, a boatman who looked as if he could belong to any age, any time.

The light from the lantern fixed to his cabin's undercarriage, which changed colour according to the weather, now turned purple. Thick heavy clouds were moving in from the east, and Atisa knew there would be rain. He pulled quickly at the rope ends, holding up the balloon. In a few moments, these dropped like a tent wall around him, and his flying machine moved up ahead, over the clouds. Looking down one last time, he remembered it was precisely this region where Gaea, his mother, had planned her exploration of the old Saka routes. Her search for these routes would begin here, in the old plateau of central India. She wanted to find the secret caves and tunnels now lost, which she believed were used by the tribe of nomadic horsemen called the Sakas more than 1800 years ago. The Sakas had made repeated forays into western and central India during the time of the Gupta rulers of north India. Soon after, they had set up their own kingdom around the city of Ujjain in the heart of the plateau. He wondered if the voice he had heard came from that time and shrugged it off. His inventor father Gesar was always cautioning him against speculation. Speculation, as Gesar sometimes said, never allows a methodical conclusion to things.

Atisa threw his head back and his hair bounced past his shoulders again. He was taller now, his head almost reached the cabin roof, from where the ropes led up to the balloon and its whorl-like folds. With his father, he had made so many changes that the flying machine little resembled the old machine that the grateful Greek inventor Daedalus had presented him. This was soon after Atisa's first adventure when he had travelled to the seven wonders of the ancient world, in search of Daedalus' lost son Icarus. He still remembered the pyramids, the old lighthouse and the mausoleum where he had finally found Icarus, safe and well, though his attempt to fly high on wings designed by his father had failed. The flying machine still had the low rounded seats and the old telescope, but it could now be folded up into a more portable object, so that it looked like an umbrella, even if an overly large, cumbersome one. Gesar had always added new things to it such as the sound catcher and a lantern whose light read the weather and changed colour accordingly. Gesar was even now working on a decoder to translate some basic words from ancient languages such as Sanskrit, Chinese, Prakrit and even

Pali, and Atisa wondered how far his father's work had gone on that. New things could always be grafted on to trusted old things, only to make them as good as new, even more long-lasting, Gesar always said.

He wanted to email Elder Lama. Perhaps he could get him to decode the message for him. His thoughts now became more serious, and Atisa decided to head homeward, hoping there were no new storms on the way.

Elder Lama's Advice

Varahamihira chose the most appropriate way to secrete away some of his more incendiary scrolls. In the last few days of his stay in Pataliputra, he had studied the stars in more detail, and his excitement and anxiety had grown in equal measure. It was a rare eclipse and an event that would be a privilege to witness. He had also made observations relating to the movement of the sun, the moon and the planets, and concluded that these had little to do with human endeavours. Yet he could not air these opinions aloud. In this time and age, it would be blasphemous. And so Varahamihira had decided on the next best thing. Till times were appropriate and people were more receptive to new truths, his knowledge would have to be hidden away.

Varahamihira had put his trust in a trader who roamed the empire, from east to west and north to south, and who traversed every route there was, even the secret ones. And to him, Varahamihira had passed on the necessary directions. The scrolls, which made up most of his new work, would for now be hidden away in a monastery far to the east, beyond the borders of Bengal, past the port of Tamralipti on the sea, located deep in Arakan.

The trader could be trusted, though Varahamihira wished he would not be so very nonchalant in his attitude. Now Varahamihira waited for his return and put off his journey to Jhansi, hoping to meet him. But it proved to be a long wait, and he grew increasingly frustrated. Varahamihira could not put off his return to Jhansi once the monsoons began. That would make travel difficult. But as days passed and the trader did not return, Varahamihira, making no secret of his disgust with the trader, made the decision to return.

Several evenings had passed since then, and a thousand and more years later, the message Atisa had copied still remained to be deciphered. Elder Lama had barely glanced at the message, for he had to suddenly leave for a monastery in Myanmar. Gesar, Atisa's father, too was already away on his new expedition, one that involved high-altitude photographing of the Himalayas. At that height, the eclipse would be an ethereal sight too. From his room, high up in the house where he lived, Atisa could see the silver roofed hangars of his father's flying school. The school was built along the mountain, looking at times like an extension of the mountain itself.

Far below, the wind tore off a kite and took it away, and he felt a similar restlessness. He thought about the message and about his mother as well. So far he had had no word from her. His mother was already in the valley of the old Narmada river, deep in the plateau that he had flown over, not too many days ago. Gaea was certain her excavations would reveal much more about the Sakas than was presently known. 'There's more to them than just being brave warriors,' she had told Atisa and his father, Gesar, as she got her equipment together. 'They travelled faster than anyone before them. They dug tunnels and rode up mountains. Oh it's fascinating...'

Perhaps she also sensed how lost Atisa would feel all alone, for she stopped to smile at him reassuringly, 'Don't worry, I will make sure you join me soon.' He remembered this conversation, longed once again to be part of his mother's adventures and dug his hands into his pockets. 'I just have to hear from her first,' he said to himself, as his fingers closed on the message that he had hastily copied down.

The machine stretched out in the yard below, its ropes creaked and whined in the wind, but this didn't alarm Atisa. All the repairs he had carried out had helped. He had flown it down to the village several times already. It had given him a chance to meet Lansik, a boy who worked as a guide and wanted to be a mountaineer. Lansik was teaching him ventriloquism, a secret known only to members of his tribe.

When Atisa looked down again past the valley, down the low rice terraces, he saw a light flashing. He stared, as the balloon bobbed and bubbled in the wind, knowing it was Lansik who was signalling to him using his pocket torch. From the manner in which the lights came on and off, Atisa guessed it was important, and he had to leave immediately. He pulled at the bellows, and the balloon rose in the wind. The cold winter breeze swept in and he turned his machine towards the village, knowing he would have to fly close over the rice terraces to reach Lansik as quickly as possible. It was a quiet short journey, and the mountains were also quiet because there were few trekkers at this time of early winter. His machine drifted down slowly towards the main square. A few people in the lone restaurant on the road smiled, and he noticed that there were some new visitors who looked at his machine curiously. A couple of girls giggled, and he was glad that the balloon's folds dropped over him as he landed. It helped hide how embarrassed he suddenly felt.

He placed a rock on the ropes, and there was Lansik waiting for him at the post office. 'What was all that hurry about?' Atisa asked.

'I am sorry, I just thought you'd want to know. There's a message.' Rummaging in his pocket, Lansik drew out yet another piece of paper. Atisa recognized Elder Lama's loping handwriting and understood right away what the message was about. Just as it had happened on many an occasion before, his teacher had read his mind and had left behind his response with Lansik. The message he had copied had been fully deciphered and written out in Elder Lama's neat hand; it was now all too easy to understand. *Please help. I have an important message and there are people who may stop me. Please help.* He read the message again, hearing Lansik speak softly, his voice mingling with the last owl calls and the sound of the crickets. He also remembered the voice as it had come over the sound catcher. 'Elder Lama gave it to my father when I went up to the mountains with them. I wished I could have gone on ahead, but father said no,' Lansik shook his head sadly.

'But why didn't Elder Lama tell me himself, before he left?' Atisa asked himself wryly, while Lansik looked puzzled. Elder Lama had added a few more lines hurriedly and more unsteadily. Perhaps he had written these standing up, balancing the note on someone's backpack or shoulder.

This is somewhat cryptic, and words are missing. It is clearly a message for help. Whoever sent it knows of some danger, and he is afraid to say more, even who he is.

Atisa drew in his breath. Something in the voice he had heard had indeed carried fear, and now Atisa remembered it all over again and shuddered. He thanked Lansik and set off for home again. He would read the note once again when he was home. But he did not know what he would do next. That lost feeling came over him again. Perhaps Elder Lama's sending it via Lansik was a way of telling him not to get too excited, to let things take their own time. Sometimes, with time, mysteries unravelled in their own way.

He was halfway up the mountains when he looked up. He saw the house standing by itself, and there was his father's study all lit up. Gesar had already left, his new invention, the language decoder, as yet unfinished. The decoder, when finished, would be able to read and decipher old voices and ancient languages. Gesar had planned to attach it to the sound catcher in Atisa's flying machine. Gesar had left earlier than scheduled with his team of mountaineers and skydivers as a period of exceptionally fine weather had set in earlier than expected. At this time, his new invention, unfinished and incomplete, was still a secret. Atisa's father almost always never revealed anything about his inventions till they were complete. He also zealously guarded them, and the inner study was always locked when he wasn't there.

It was only Atisa who had been offered a sneak preview of the language decoder. It looked very much like a belt worn by a tribal chief, and Atisa hadn't been much impressed, though he kept his thoughts to himself.

'It is a necessary addition for your sound catcher,' Gesar had said. The sound catcher had also been designed by him. At first it had been a cumbersome box-like thing, but over time, Gesar had made it more polished and portable. And now there was this strange device shaped like a belt that would alter the sound catcher even more. Atisa flung back his red-gold hair as it fell over his forehead and eyes. He was impatient now as he ran down the long corridor towards the study. When he opened the door, he saw that the room looked just as it did every day.

He frowned. He knew for sure the room hadn't been disturbed. You could make that out, for everything was in its place, in perfect order. The chair stood against the wall, the cushions on the armchair rigid and expectant, and the floor wore no sign of being stepped on. The old floor tiles always gave away even the faintest imprint of anything. Only the flowers in the vase drooped a bit more as the wind rushed in from the open door, but he was certain that no one had been there. Still, when he pulled open his father's secret work drawer, using the code only a few were privy to, he found that the belt wasn't there.

He looked thoughtful as he returned once more to the open grounds and wondered if his father had somehow taken it with him to work on. There was nothing Atisa could do till he heard from him. For the night, the flying machine would rest in its hangar. Tomorrow would be another day, he thought, another exciting day.

The Decoder

A tisa slept poorly, in spite of the fact that he had fallen asleep a bit too early over the book of vampires set in the time of the king Chandragupta Vikramaditya. It was a book he had begun reading and longed to finish soon, for it was all about magicians and sorcerers who used vampires and flying genies to carry out their evil tasks. Some of them were even employed as the state's officers, and some were used by evil people for evil means as well. Atisa had found it all fascinating.

In his sleep, he had dreamt about a vampire who was teaching him the skills of ventriloquism, just as Lansik had been doing. But this vampire also had the ability to read people's minds and was mischievous enough to reveal their deepest secrets out loud, especially things they would rather keep hidden. And Atisa found himself in his dream chased by too many people, all of whom had become his enemies just in the course of one dream, and all thanks to the vampire, his teacher. No one likes his darkest thoughts being made public, and even if Atisa's new abilities now showed up a lot of evil people, there were those who were now his bitterest enemies. They would stop at nothing to get him. Atisa saw himself being chased through forests, down the streets of an old-looking city, into tunnels that led through deep mountains, and all the time he heard footsteps behind. He knew he would soon be caught, and he woke up with a start when an arrow rushed deceptively slowly past him. To his relief, as his breath slowed down, he realized it was the soft breeze that came up from the valley in the morning. Lansik had shown him the stones that were critical to the art of ventriloquism. Lansik had received these from a vendor who came over the mountains every once in a while, especially when the passes were free of snowmelt. These were special stones that allowed you to make all kinds of secret calls, for ventriloquism was a skill favoured by ancient warriors to deceive the enemy.

A wind had come in during the night, and the balloon was now spread over the backyard, with the cabin stuck fast to the doors of the hangar. Its colourful patches shone in the mild sun. Its silver panels gleamed. Atisa had patched the cloth making up the balloon several times already, and now the cabin inside was as comfortable as a small cottage. As the machine lay prone, the weather lantern lolled like a giant butterfly, its light now a pale blue.

Atisa remembered things from the night before: the missing belt, Elder Lama's message and how much he hoped to receive a message from his mother any moment. He stood at the window, trying to work on throwing his sound, as ventriloquists did. He was pleased at his success when a starling nearby looked up too surprised and just as quickly flew away.

Morning passed quickly as Atisa realized that working the air bellows on the balloon wasn't much fun. These were the modifications on the machine that he had planned – balloon-like wheels tethered to the end of the machine so it could take better advantage of the wind. It was only when he was checking his cabin that he stopped short startled, for his father's unfinished decoder, missing the night before, was in the inside cabinet. He picked it up gingerly, and then rummaging inside, he found also a few pages of a user manual Gesar had left behind, bound in tape. It was the most unusual thing his father could have done, for his father hated writing out things.

Looking at the decoder now, Atisa saw it was more than just a strange-looking belt. It had two ends that he had to fit in like earphones. Reading the notes, he could almost hear his father's voice just as it had sounded the day he had explained the basics to Atisa.

It's an automated language decoder, and especially of use to you, since you have been in one too many adventures to my liking, Gesar had written. The words often ran into each other and Atisa smiled, realizing his father's enthusiasm once he had finally made the decoder work. *It will decode some basic words and make it easier for you, especially if you find yourself in a strange place or with someone you are unable to understand.*

As he read Gesar's next words, Atisa saw that they were like an answer to his question. *Do you know how a conversation between two people begins? Yes, with some basics. It's those essential words in every old language that this decoder can translate effectively for you. Try it and see.*

Atisa tightened the belt around himself and fixed the two loping loose ends to his ears. It made him feel somewhat like an alien, but no sooner had he put it on than the belt came to life.

He heard Elder Lama's voice wish him in Chinese and then speaking in other languages too. Elder Lama knew several languages, not just Sanskrit and Chinese, but also the ancient languages such as Aramaic, Akkadian and old Persian. He was even familiar with Latin and some of the old Celtic languages of Europe.

Then he was startled to hear his father's voice in his ears, and Gesar sounded pleased like a happy schoolboy, as he finished off after Elder Lama. 'Now, if you find yourself in a strange land and you have no idea how far back in time you have gone, maybe this will help you.'

'There are just a few sentences and essential words that I've fed into it. It has a robotic memory and will work when it has to. Now you have a portable sound catcher and a portable, wearable, even if distinctly unfashionable, decoder.'

Atisa grinned as if he could imagine his father's face, 'Oh yes, that's quite a lot to wear.'

He was just putting away the decoder's earphones, when the sound catcher picked up the sound of jingling bells and a distinct prolonged trilling. The time for the yak herds to make their way down the valley was still some weeks away, and so Atisa was curious as to who it could be.

The Trader's Visit

Atisa looked through his telescope and saw nothing at first but the straggly bare trees and the few cyclists going up the valley road. Then he picked up the dots, all moving in an orderly line. He heard again that distinct unmusical calling. It was a procession of slow-moving animals, and he didn't realize it was all part of a trader's entourage till it arrived almost at his doorstep, several minutes later.

The new arrival led his animals into the monastery grounds next door, and Atisa noticed he had a cheeky square face, half hidden by a wide conical hat. He wore a cloak that reached his knees, of the same grey-black colour as his beard, and the bagpipe he played lay over his shoulders like a tropical snake.

'I am Nurah the trader.' And he blew through his pipe almost as if he were welcoming his own arrival – *tum tum tum*.

And the flying machine responded as the wind flew into its folds, *whoosh*...

The trader said that Elder Lama had sent him. 'I was to drop off pounds of butter at the monastery, but I have a long way to go.' He spoke in a matter-of-fact manner but in several disjointed sentences.

He pointed to his yaks and Atisa saw they all carried baskets, two on each side, so that the animals were not weighed down, but it made them look like very oversized yaks indeed. Nurah gestured dramatically, 'All things in these baskets are precious. They have my telescopes and glasses and also kites. There's a major eclipse due, a rare event. Very rare indeed.' He paused, as if to convince himself about this, before he went on. 'What's unusual is that the moon will be closer to the earth than it has ever been in ten or, maybe, twelve centuries, and then another planet, perhaps Mars, will be perfectly aligned with it, so that all three are in a straight line. It will be almost as if they are saluting the sun...' He took off his hat, looked inside it and put it back on, looking worried. 'So bad things could happen but also good ones, who knows. There are also these almanacs, to show the exact moment it will happen,' he said pointing to his sack. And he looked down at himself, and Atisa saw his cloak pockets bulging out with palm leaf scrolls tied up with a thin silken thread. 'Maybe there are things I can offer you.' He looked expectantly at Atisa, who regretfully shook his head. The man went on as if he hadn't noticed. 'There are lots of things to prove in the eclipse, and an astronomer wants all this stuff so he can study the eclipse. I have to get all this stuff to him in time, else... the king will have my hide, cancel my licence.' He went on, not stopping when Atisa tried to interrupt him. Did he really mention a king? But he was speaking so fast that Atisa couldn't be certain, and he realized he had to get back to his unfinished work on the flying machine. 'The astronomer has to prove something, something he has discovered on his own... that this event will occur only once in two thousand years.'

Nurah paused and thought over what he had just said, and he went on. 'Well, give or take a few hundred years. And the moon will be closer to the earth than ever before. But I think I told you this, didn't I? So close that you could almost see its mountains and craters and tunnels, and if you were to stand on the high mountains, you could almost jump and land on it...'

He chortled at the thought. 'Except that you wouldn't perhaps land too safely on it, the law of gravity being what it is there,' pointed out Atisa, in a way he hoped that didn't sound too rude.

Nurah looked puzzled. He frowned and said 'Eh?' but Atisa turned to his drawings that he had secured to the ground. On long sheets of paper, he had sketched how the machine would look with its new balloon wheels attached underneath, but the wind kept tearing the paper with his sketches away. He had thought of rectangle-shaped balloons that he would fix to the ends just below his small cabin, and these would open and swell up gradually at the press of a button. He hoped that would make his machine look like a spaceship. The trader, however, did not mind when Atisa, gathering up the papers hurriedly, did not explain again. Instead he got interested in the machine.

'Maybe the astronomer would be interested in something like that. He could see the moon and the eclipse up close. Never really have I seen a machine like this.' 'It isn't on sale,' said Atisa a bit coldly, but the man only grinned. He put his hat on more securely on his head and walked all around the machine, murmuring to himself, as his yaks milled around. They were well-behaved yaks, Atisa couldn't help noticing, for they did not move to the garden and always looked up when the trader blew sharply once on his pipe.

'I have these kites,' the trader now said, 'that could work just as well as your balloons.' Atisa stopped, looking up at him doubtfully. 'These are dragon-shaped kites. You know, you can unwind this spool and they spread out really fast, and then they drink in air and fly.'

'And they are made of stiff tent cloth. I got them,' said the trader, 'from those who came from the old Mongol lands, far away in the mountains. It will make your machine look like a dragon chariot.' 'Yes it will. Believe me,' said Nurah when he saw the scepticism spread on Atisa's face, 'and the strangest thing is that the material takes in the colour of things around it. So when you are up in the clouds, it will take on the colours of sunset or sunrise. Of course,' he grinned sheepishly, 'it's not going to be much visible at night, for all things then turn black but,' and now he shrugged, 'there is not much you can do with the night. Why not try it?'

And so Atisa did, and a few minutes later, he couldn't help but look pleased at how the machine looked with the kites attached. The trader smiled and his eyes crinkled up. 'The new wheels do look good, don't they?'

'Yes,' said Atisa, 'except that it does take time to fix it all up.' He shifted the kites so they were placed more effectively to pick up the wind. 'Why not try flying it now?' suggested Nurah. Atisa worked at the bellows, lifting it so the wind rushed in at the bottom, and in moments the kites had spread themselves, fluttering as they gulped in the air. The balloon whooshed and was swept away so fast that Atisa found himself, machine and all, in the nearest copse of trees, quite unable to extricate himself.

'Oh dear, well the first time is always tricky,' said the trader shaking his head, 'we will get you out in no time.'

He was running his fingers through his beard, and then all at once, he began bellowing out to his yaks. 'Stop, stop, you might disturb the old monks,' said Atisa, but despite his worry and irritation, he couldn't help being amazed. The trader handed over the ends of the trailing machine ropes to the yaks and commanded them, at the call of his bagpipe, to fall into four lines. In no time, the yaks had pulled out the time machine, working in perfect unison and rhythm. 'We seem to have wasted some time, I am sorry,' the trader said, doffing his long hat. 'I am sorry too, for making a fuss,' said Atisa, but

Nurah the trader grinned and waved his apology aside. 'You know I have these other fancy kites too,' he said instead. 'You have these special glow-worms attached to leaves fixed on to the kite, and you can see things in the darkest of places like caves and tunnels.' He insisted that Atisa accept one of the kites as if in apology for all that had happened. 'Believe me, you might find it handy one day. In fact, I am certain you will.' There was something in the way he said this that puzzled Atisa, but Nurah was whistling a moment later, gathering in his herd. The yaks had been sitting patiently under trees, resting after the unexpected exercise they were suddenly part of. 'Must go now,' he said, taking off his hat, and then he struggled to put it back on, looking suddenly confused. 'Varaha...,' he broke off, shaking his head. 'Varaha... I keep forgetting the name of the astronomer. Never mind. Once I reach Pataliputra, I will ask for him.'

Nurah was such a funny, old-fashioned man, Atisa thought, watching him depart. He used old names for everything and had such old stuff with him too. He knew his father would like to meet him. And then, as he suddenly remembered something, the trader trotted back towards him, holding tight on to the yak he was sitting on. It was as if his thoughts too would vanish if he loosened his grip in any manner. 'That's your father I saw over the mountains. Quite a high leap from the plane. I'd have taken a picture, but there are some things spoiled by a photo. And anyway I was headed here, so thought I would tell you anyway.' 'Yes, I have been hoping to hear from him,' Atisa replied, 'and from my mom too...' 'Oh, it's so hot.' And Atisa wasn't sure if Nurah had said that or one of his yaks, for that was when the sound catcher burst to life. He rushed towards it. Twice before, he had heard his father's voice, but it had broken away. Sometimes on high altitudes, wireless connectivity was difficult. 'Now what is that noise?'

asked Nurah looking at nothing in particular, but his pretence seemed a bit deliberate, for the sound of the catcher picking up was like a pecking, quite like a woodpecker at work, and this meant that the message was urgent. It was his father's secret code. Soon it would take on more urgency, a louder note, like someone chopping wood. Nurah looked at Atisa curiously. 'That bird has come here too early, I think. You are not a ventriloquist, are you?'

Atisa lied desperately, hoping no one at the monastery would overhear him. 'That's an irritable monk. Perhaps he is just clearing his throat.'

Nurah looked at him a bit reproachfully, 'You are not very good at lying. Besides, you know, I have masks you can wear over your face that change your moods. And no one can tell if you are lying, for a lie will appear as the truth.' He frowned for he had confused himself, 'or whatever... really.'

Atisa shook his head in amusement. But the man now turned, calling out to his yaks. The sound catcher was now quiet. No sound emanated from it. He waited for the green light that showed his father had left a message. But the light didn't come on, and he hesitated. That was unusual. Why had his father been so secretive? And why had the yak trader been so curious?

When there were too many open-ended questions, you could tell there was an adventure brewing. He wished he was more certain. He didn't want to chase the wrong clue.

To his relief, the sound catcher burst to life soon after, and there was his father, and Atisa couldn't wait to get started. 'Was it you who had been trying to get through?'

For only his parents had the special transmitters that allowed them to send messages to the sound catcher, wherever they were. But his father didn't make his usual joke about the sound catcher being as bad as a telephone; instead he sounded cautious, 'Yes, I had to be careful,' and it was most unlike Gesar to be this way. Atisa could hear the wind and the slow-moving ice at the other end. His father's voice was now breaking off, and Atisa realized that Gesar was perhaps moving higher on his glider. He leant closer to catch his father's every word. 'There was the matter of a small theft,' Gesar said. 'Some cameras are missing.'

'Oh dad,' and this was all Atisa could say. He knew Gesar was upset.

'I have some backups and we will make do with the other cameras, but it happened when we were at the foothills, so it could have been anyone. It could have been a rival team that is trying to set the same record.' Gesar's team of skydivers that had been training all year round were now preparing to fly over the Everest and execute a spectacular dive from that height. It was a move that had attracted a lot of attention, as it would coincide with the great eclipse. Gesar's team had special overhead cameras that would enable them to take spectacular photographs of the mountains and the eclipse. Gesar had fitted the cameras with special lenses that would take clear pictures even in uncertain weather conditions, and some had exceptional zoom-in qualities. There was silence, apart from the flutter and crack of high winds, and some odd booming noises as planes broke the sound barrier. Atisa could hear the quiet timeless sound of snow falling. Atisa desperately wanted to help Gesar any way he could. 'I just wanted to tell you,' said Gesar. 'We will still manage to set our records; only, we won't have good photos to take.' He stopped before he spoke in a far firmer tone, 'Have you heard from your mother?'

'No, I haven't yet.' And Atisa went on, missing the worry in his father's voice, 'I wish I was there with you.' 'There is always another time.' There was a silence before Gesar went on, 'Actually, more than the loss of my cameras, it's the fact that you haven't heard from Gaea that's worrying me. It's time you should have.'

'And what...' 'Let's wait for a day or two,' his father interrupted, 'and then I will fly to where Elder Lama is and ask if he could help. He would know something about those ancient routes or the particular paths the Sakas used.' 'Can't I go instead?'

'Atisa...,' said his father with a sigh. It was heartfelt, and he realized that his father had too much on his mind. Unable to do anything, and still wishing he could go to meet his father, he flew around with his machine as the evening sun set. He hadn't even been able to tell his father that he would have felt more useful if he had been with him.

The Priest from Long Ago

Atisa was pleased to see that the new kites indeed worked well. The trader had been right, for the kites caught the light and changed colour in accordance. Besides, they made a pleasing sound against the wind, as he flew hoping to test them out. Still he couldn't help feeling curious. How come Nurah had known so much about what his father had been up to? He couldn't have gone far now with his yak herds, but yet he had vanished.

He turned the decoder around on his head, and wished there was a way of making it look less obvious. If he let his long hair cover his ears, maybe the long earplugs would not be so visible. When he heard the crackle break through suddenly on his sound catcher, he quickly became very alert. The special light was on, and this time it could only be his mother. Next, he heard a distinct scratching, and in growing excitement, he raised the amplifier. He tried zooming into a location, tracking the sound, and then he couldn't believe it. He heard the same noises he had heard not too long ago, the neighing of horses or something similar, the jingling of bells and the cheeping of birds. And for a wild moment, Atisa thought it was the travelling salesman again with his herd of yaks. Then he heard the clear sound of temple bells, an owl calling and the musical sound of a waterfall. He bent closer, wondering why, if it was his mother, she wasn't speaking up.

'Mom, are you there?' When he couldn't hear a thing,

he got frantic and pressed his ear close to the sound catcher, wondering in some desperation if there was something he could do. And then a voice crackled through. It wasn't his mother but someone who at first said something that made no sense. At first, Atisa couldn't understand the language. Someone was speaking much too fast and so with shaking hands, he switched on the decoder. Miraculously, in a few moments, the decoder, with a click, began working, just as his father had said, and the words came to life. *In the name of all holy gods, there is an injured man here.* Instantly Atisa knew that this was a voice different from the one he had heard before, but it held the same urgency. And though this was something he had not expected to hear, he waited, his heart beating fast. He felt his breath growing more and more ragged, and the wind pushed his hair against his face, but he didn't care. He hoped the voice wouldn't break away this time, or that it wouldn't be totally undecipherable. The man appeared to break out into sobs, loud hiccups that broke through the sound catcher, when he spoke. *An injured man. And my temple is a place for healing, but this man is in a bad shape.*

Atisa understood that the man was a priest and that he was talking of something or someone in his temple. His voice was hoarse, he was panting, and it was clear that he was nervous and also immensely tired. *I'd never have done this. But those men on horses riding by every day make me afraid. They ride by with such force that I fear one day...*

The man went on, gulping. Atisa could hear his desperate breathing on the sound catcher and knew for sure that he meant the Sakas. *I am speaking through this box. This very strange thing that makes me forget all that I learnt at the feet of my forefathers, and now may I be cursed by my ancestors. An injured man has been left behind. I was told that if I talk through this, help would come.* There was a pause. His quick breathing could be heard over the sound catcher, and then the man asked the question he should have asked at the very beginning: *Are you Atisa?* Atisa jumped at that. There could be no doubt now that his mother indeed had something to do with this. *Yes.*

He wondered if the amplifier could even pick up the sound of his heart thumping fast and erratically. *Is she safe? My mother?* His words sounded desperate, and at the silence that stretched at the other end, he felt his lips turn dry and his hands were clammy on the ropes. Amazingly, the decoder picked his word up, that one word he uttered – mother – and translated it for the benefit of someone listening from another age. *Oh,* he heard the profound sigh of relief. *I was thinking it's a mere block of stone, and now I find it is indeed miraculous. I have a reply. I hear a voice.* The man laughed more in his nervousness. *A woman, she's your mother, I understand now. She insisted I call you. Because... because there is a man dying. And she said you must come. You must.* After that there was nothing. The voice had lost itself in a faraway time.

He heard the wind and the metallic, rhythmic sound of temple bells again, and from their jangling, Atisa could tell something was shaking them fiercely. There was perhaps a gale on, and he heard the sound of falling rocks, the hiss of a snake and it was all swept away by someone playing the bagpipe.

He looked around and realized he had flown far too close to the ground. His attention had been so riveted on the sound catcher that he had missed pulling at the ropes or steering the machine away from the road. To his relief, he was somewhere in the main town square, a place he was familiar with, and there was Nurah looking at him bemused and in his usual friendly way. 'I am trying to remember his name, the astronomer's,' he said sheepishly, 'and thought I'd take a little more time on it.' This time he had only a few of his yaks with him. And Atisa wondered why he had not heard him. Or did the sound catcher block out every other noise, when it received one particular message? It puzzled him, and he thought he would ask his father about it later. 'You need to go there, don't you?' Nurah looked towards the machine and nodded again somewhere to the west. It seemed he did know where the voice had come from. 'Yes. But how do you know?'

'I have these ear trumpets, you know,' he said, taking off his cap and showing him cones stuck into his ears. 'They help me hear things I am not supposed to...' He shrugged nonchalantly before going on. 'The same astronomer..., I thought I'd impress him with these. And I wanted to get these to him before the great eclipse happens. But I just can't remember his name, so how do I tell him?' He looked up in the sky, took off his hat and scratched his head for answers, but his forgetfulness persisted and Atisa was very intrigued. 'I can hear you too, especially if the wind is strong. My trumpets will catch your balloon noise, and my telescopes will see your light. So just move it, you must go fast.' Nurah seemed to know far more than he was letting on. Atisa knew that he should be wary, but getting to his mother was also urgent. 'You should start by nightfall, then the wind will pick up and you can go fast.'

Atisa though couldn't wait till evening. He was worried about his mother, and his hands on the ropes were so still that the balloon wobbled and shook. What exactly had the priest said? His mother had left the transmitter with him so he could pass on the message. In that case, where was his mother? With his heart beating fast, and looking down at the earth spread below him, he hoped nothing would stop him reaching the place the man had called from. He had to find out what had happened to his mother.

Next morning, no sooner had the greyness appeared in the skies, and the golden bulbs of the monastery had been turned off, than Atisa revved his machine up. It was cumbersome, working the bellows up, stretching the kites and waiting for the weather lantern to turn a perfect blue before he knew it was just right for the flying machine to take off. He zoomed along the road at an exhilarating speed, and the first birds out in the morning scattered in alarm. He heard too the welcome sounds of the kites fluttering open under his feet, and he saw them spread out like wings in no time. He was fast nearing the point where the ground slid away. And then he was soaring high. He could see the clouds scudding past and hear the fast-moving wind, and then he saw, like faint moving dots in the horizon, the last of the yak herds. He wondered how they moved so fast. As he rose higher into the mountains, he realized he had forgotten to tell his father about the strange message he had received and also that he had at last heard of his mother.

Sliding through air, he saw the lantern change its colour, and the balloon roared as it filled with air and swelled up to double its size and then still more. The wind surged in, and it seemed there were several hundred drummers inside its folds as the wind swished and danced inside. Atisa found himself moving along at a speed faster than he had imagined. The air around him whirred and spun, the sky shook and trembled. He remembered the priest's words and knew he had to head westwards. The setting moon appeared often, waxing and waning as he picked his way through the clouds, bobbing his way through them. The balloon was like a sleigh, and the new kites helped. He passed the last flocks of migrating birds, and when he looked down below with Daedalus' telescope, there was no sign of the trader and his yaks. The strong winds that accosted him a few miles later were no surprise. He knew these could blow him away off course, and so he pulled in the ropes, drawing them in around his cabin. In this fashion, he tried to lose height gradually, but settling down to a steady pace was difficult. Atisa soon found himself low over a river. Its waves rose high and fell over the rails of his flying machine, spraying his telescope. Not too far away, a herd of elephants swam across, shying away in alarm as he passed. All he could hope for was that he hadn't gone too far off course, and as he slowed down, stopping by a copse of trees to check his surroundings, he saw the men on horseback. Shadowy outlines in that early morning, Atisa saw them racing furiously down a dusty road, and he sneezed as the dust rose high. He moved quickly back up into the clouds, hoping he had not drawn their attention, and he saw them again, a few hundred miles later. They couldn't have ridden so fast, and he knew at once, the realization hitting him with a jolt, that they were all Saka horsemen, who were riding purposefully somewhere and with intent. He knew he had to be careful and that he had travelled back into the past faster than he had anticipated.

Flying over the forests, with his lantern guiding him, he saw the grey plateau loom ahead. He knew he had to fly low and also slow down, for he was afraid of missing the priest's signal.

The earth just below had turned purple, thanks to his weather lantern. It was cold, as evening now set in far too quickly, and he shivered. He could see the silver ribbon of a small river nearby. When he amplified the sound catcher, he could hear again the sound of horses, and looking down, he saw the slow-burning campfires. Something about the arrangement warned him that he was near a soldiers' camp. He caught the faint sound of laughter and the sound of animals, and then peering ahead, looking through his telescope, he finally saw a light blinking in the forest. Atisa was certain that this was right where the voice had come from only a day ago. He remembered the priest's broken voice and harsh breathing, and the gooseflesh stood up on his arms. His sound catcher had picked up the distinct sounds of bells tolling. Straining to look into the darkness, Atisa caught his breath. He had spotted a nervous-looking priest waiting on the steps leading to a temple, his lantern held up high, to guide him safely down.

Atisa descended slowly, keeping the temple, as it stood amid a copse of trees, in sight. 'She did tell me you would need help coming in,' explained the priest within moments as he came up, his lantern bouncing unevenly as he ran towards Atisa. He helped Atisa draw his machine in and watched with fascination as Atisa folded it all up to make a neat square umbrella, wrapped up in a belt. The priest sounded breathless, but at least now that he was up close, Atisa could follow him clearly. Now as he saw him more clearly in the lantern light, he realized that the priest couldn't be much older than he was. Atisa had turned fourteen just last summer and surmised that the priest must be twenty years or so. 'I am glad I saw you clearly and that was a safe place to land,' the priest went on as he led the way back, 'but we should be careful.' He was now speaking much too fast, and Atisa quickly slipped on the earphones of the language decoder. The priest's words now came to him in Elder Lama's stentorian voice.

'I am afraid, because though this temple is too deep in the forests, the Sakas are a fierce lot. They are brave and unmatched in war. They killed the king Rudrasena, the son-in-law of the great Vikramaditya. Princess Prabhavati, Vikramaditya's daughter, needs help. And there is no way to get the news across to Pataliputra. And all I have now is an injured man, who is very sick too.' Now he spoke in broken tones, barely mouthing the words in his distress. He held the lantern high as they reached the temple, and Atisa noted the look of pride on his face as the priest pointed to it. 'This temple, do you see the beautiful stone carvings? King Vikramaditya's father, the great Samudragupta, built it for my grandfather. The king learnt the veena from my grandfather when he stopped here during his campaigns. The place filled him with peace.' It was the most fascinating temple Atisa had ever been in. It seemed to grow out of the plateau and had long, winding steps that led down to the river. There were sculptures depicting various gods and goddesses as well as scenes of everyday life on the walls. 'It was all done in a matter of days. It rained and we had to go down to the village. No one could come up here for days and when we returned, it was done. No one had any idea who had done it.'

A Message from His Mother

The priest was quite in a rush to make Atisa comfortable. He indicated a well standing in the dark moss-covered courtyard. A brass bell swung on its rope across two columns. The bell now swung in the wind, and that snuffed out immediately the small candle he had lit in the portico. It made the priest smile apologetically.

He spoke in the difficult Sanskrit Atisa had heard before. Atisa rubbed his ears where the decoder pressed really hard, and the priest drawing in his breath, continued in a low, gentle tone, 'I will speak slowly, and perhaps you might understand.' He had a young, serene, unlined face. It was hard to imagine he had been scared, and the priest, as if reading his mind, smiled. 'I am Vasudeva, educated to be a priest. Sometimes I go down to the river, and that night was particularly dark. And I was just sitting there on the steps, when it all happened.' He smiled, looking abashed suddenly. 'I am perhaps not a priest who can give up the world. My family lives in the village of Udayapuri. I came away, still not knowing what it was I really wanted. My brothers are soldiers. But I was always considered a coward.'

Atisa smiled. It sounded so familiar. He knew people at his father's flying school who had taken a year off to find themselves. The priest shrugged, 'It's hard being alone anyway, so I am glad you are here.' He was lost in thought before he pulled himself up again. 'That night when I came down to the river, it was late and I couldn't sleep.' In fact, he laughed and held up the light, and Atisa saw the tired lines now on his young face and realized he must have been waiting for him for a long time. The priest yawned now, a very polite yawn, which he tried hard to clamp down on before he began again. 'There was really no one here. This was an abandoned ghat, close to the cemetery. I thought I had never been scared before, but that place, that time...'

He shivered, drawing his shawl more closely around himself. 'There are spooks, genies, vampires and *vetals,* I mean the ghouls who roam graveyards and cemeteries, but I try hard to conquer such fears. And that was when I saw the boat. Then I saw her too.' His voice died away and Atisa held his breath. He too remembered the book on vampires he had been recently reading. 'I was nervous. I didn't expect to see anyone, let alone hear a woman's voice, and I thought it was an evil spirit. She had her hands cupped over her face, and that made her voice loud and hollow at the same time. It even had an echo...'

He laughed nervously, 'She held up a small lantern, and it made the colour of her face change, sometimes white, sometimes grey.'

Atisa smiled, and he was glad he was unseen. The candle had blown itself out and they were now in the darkness, their voices a reassurance to each other. 'I'd have turned and run, but I gripped my stick and waited. There was something about the voice. And in that faint light of the moon, I saw the boat floundering. Moving up and down on the rocks, the water swirled and turned silver. I waded in, and that was when above her voice, I heard him moan. It took me time to reach them though...'

He shivered, hiding his face in his hands, and Atisa waited for him to continue. 'There was a man in the boat, and I could see he was injured and he looked very weak. He breathed in a ragged way. I could see the bruises on his feet and arms and the gash on his forehead.' There was just a brief hesitation before the priest went on again. It struck Atisa that he was taking his time, deliberating over what to say next. 'And he was delirious and moaning. We were both alarmed the sound would carry. But we were lucky the wind had died down by then, else we would have surely been heard by the Sakas on the hilltop and all around. She said, "I found him in the forests, and he did not know who had attacked him. It happened just as he had headed out on the road westward on his horse, and he had barely managed to escape with his life." But she said she had to leave. She rubbed her arms and bent across the boat, suddenly tired. I understood she must have rowed a long time. We somehow managed to drag the boat up behind the rocks. It was all heavy work, with that wounded man inside. And that was when the riders appeared, like black shadows overhead.'

He pointed up, and Atisa saw the sharp line of the ravines. 'They had appeared on the quiet, sounding like sudden blasts of thunder, and so we waited. The lantern went out with a last flash of blue, and then it was all black around us. We waited for what must have been a long, long time, and then she said she had to get away fast and asked if I could help. She had to travel further herself. And so I told her about the horse, the one left by a trader who sometimes passes by.'

Did Atisa imagine it, or was there a hesitation in his voice again? Vasudeva coughed repeatedly before he went on, as if he had to look for the right words. 'The boat would draw attention, because the rivers were being patrolled all the time by the Sakas. She would ride through the forests, she said, and I begged her to wait the night. But there were the Saka warriors on their horses, already watchful and waiting. We could see them, but they did not know. The two of us took the injured man via a small narrow path, back to the temple.'

Looking up, as the priest neared the end of his story, Atisa saw with a start that the soldiers had appeared again. He could hear their tired horses stomping on the stones; there were tapers and torches dying on the ravines, and sometimes stray voices reached them too. The priest rose from the temple steps where they had been sitting and hoped the sound of the boat lapping on the waters would not be heard. 'It took us a long time. And he's still delirious. We had a hard time getting him in. It was a wonder the Sakas didn't find him. Now I am worried about the boat. The clouds will clear by tomorrow, and the boat will give us away.'

Vasudeva scanned the skies with some anxiety. He looked anxious to hurry back. The injured man who lay in one corner of the temple's inner room was now unconscious, and as they sat in the courtyard, thinking over what to do, Atisa heard him groaning again. The priest hurried back to the man in the inner room. He lay bundled up in a blanket with low-burning candles all about him. Atisa wanted to know more about his mother, but all the priest knew was that she had gone off on his horse. 'She was in a hurry, and I begged her to take a message to the princess. But she had to go. Someone had promised to show her a way to the north-west.' Why was it important for a message to be passed to the princess? wondered Atisa.

But the priest had turned to tend to his patient, pounding a mix of herb and leaves that had the faint smell of basil. Atisa knew he had to go and look for the boat. There was every chance that in the clear light of day, it could give them all away. He found it within moments after he walked out, stepping gingerly along the narrow space between the forest and the river. He had been alerted by the soft sound of water lapping against wood and the bobbing sounds the boat made every time it moved. He waded through the damp undergrowth, brushed against the weeds and found the boat caught in the tall grass, and then to his surprise, he heard a familiar ticking noise; it was his mother's transmitter, the one the priest had used as well to send a message to him. It was obvious from the light that blinked on and off that his mother too had left a message for him. It was an old-fashioned machine, designed by his father. It came with a lever that had to be pulled up to get it working and a tiny microphone that crackled in the wind. He couldn't imagine what the soldiers, if they had found it, would have made of it. But to his welcome relief, he heard her voice the moment he cranked up the lever. There was a pause and when her voice came next, he could tell she was looking over her shoulder as she talked quickly and in short bursts, and her voice ebbed and fell every time the wind broke in. 'It was too unsafe where I was. There was an old map I had that showed me a place where the old Saka routes began. But barely had I begun exploring when I realized that someone was on my trail. Believe it or not, it was a man on wings.'

He gasped at what he had just heard and at the amazement and fear in his mother's voice. 'At first, it did look as if he had a way of swinging from branch to branch, but he had on a pair of wings, triangular and silken, embedded it seemed with glow-worms all over.' *Glow-worms*. He listened to his mother again and remembered the kites Nurah had described to him.

'It was just in time that I fell through the crack in the plateau. It was just a gap and I thought I could jump across, but instead I found someone there who led me through a secret route in it. He was someone I'd come across again later. That route inside the plateau shortens the distance from Pataliputra to Ujjain in the west, a city just beyond the plateau. When we came up a short distance later, we were in a village. It looked just like villages of the present, unchanged with time. The man who led me there said he would return.

To cut a long story short, the eclipse is due and just like very many places in our time too, people have always been fearful of eclipses. But it was the nature of the fear I saw everywhere that told me I was in a strange place...'

He heard his mother draw her breath in sharply before she went on, 'and in a stranger time too. The man had warned me that I looked different and villagers suspected me. In times of fear, people are more afraid and willing to believe in rumours. At the inn where I stopped, I told them I was a magician, but there would be always someone or other at my door, or outside, keeping an eye. And looking down from my window, I saw the man with wings once again.' He shivered as Gaea's voice died away. Suddenly it seemed the man with wings was there again.

What happened? He said it aloud, almost as if he were conversing with her. He waited. The transmitter ticked on, and it took his mother a long time to speak up again. Atisa was proud of his mother, the strange places she went to and the wonderful things she did, but for the first time he felt the twinges of anxiety about her. They had often found themselves lost in time and had always been confident of returning, but what if things didn't work out? What if they did get lost? It wasn't fun to get lost forever.

He heard his mother take a deep breath before she continued. 'One afternoon, two days later, I did hear a tapping under my floor. I pushed aside the mat and found a trapdoor and my rescuer of the day before under it. So down the ladder and into another tunnel we went. He revealed by way of introduction that he was one of the pathfinders, the tribe that led warriors and others in need through secret routes. They also knew the dark and hidden routes through the forest. He said he needed my help more than I needed his.' Atisa heard his mother's quick indrawn laughter. 'And on the way he said he had to get an injured man to safety. But he couldn't go all the way, for he had to warn someone else, a princess far away on the west coast. It was suddenly all very mysterious. "Don't worry," he kept telling me. "Someone will be waiting for you." But he was pleading and led me to the man, and I saw how serious his injuries were. I got him to the priest, not a minute too late. It was a surreal experience, the priest waiting, with his old flickering lantern in the darkness all around. It was just as the pathfinder had said.'

Atisa wondered... The priest had looked tired, and it seemed now he had been waiting for a while. Was it the injured man he had been waiting for? Was he hiding more than he was letting on? And why had a message to be passed on to the princess so very urgently?

Atisa pulled the boat back on to land and covered it with weeds, and the priest looked happy to have him back. 'Thank god, you are safe. I was worried the Sakas would notice you.' 'But are they all dangerous?' Atisa hadn't realized he had asked the question aloud. He was certain he had been seen; besides he had not been exactly quiet. There had been a sudden lull, and he was worried his mother's voice had carried. And while he heard the horses neighing very close, nothing had happened; no one had sounded the alarm notifying everyone of his presence. The silence had only stretched, and after a while the warriors had moved away with their horses. The priest looked puzzled by the question, and he floundered for an answer. 'Some of them do have a reputation, especially after one of their leaders swore a lifelong enmity to our king Chandragupta after the Saka king was killed right in his camp by our king in disguise, because he had dared demand the queen as ransom. And then they killed his son-in-law, the king Rudrasena, in revenge.'

The priest shrugged, somehow unwilling to tell the whole story. The sick man was moaning in pain and still delirious. And walking away, the priest said over his shoulder to Atisa, 'But it's been some years, and they are now much weakened. But a reputation, good or bad, can be hard to shake off.' The priest provided him a simple lunch of hard bread and vegetables, and there were bananas too. 'Whatever I could spare from the elephant herds, that is,' he grinned ruefully. 'At least the Sakas are afraid of them too.' Later that afternoon, when he had finished offering his prayers to the god, the priest suggested to Atisa that he wait for the trader. 'He is expected any time really. Usually he comes once in a moon cycle, and he can take you to Ujjain. It is a big city, and perhaps you would know soon about your mother.' He looked apologetically at Atisa, spreading his hands wide in explanation, 'I have to be here and keep him safe. It is important that his presence is not given away.'

The injured man was now asleep, and it was a welcome sign, even though a small one, that he was recovering. The priest had treated him with some medicine and he was no longer delirious. Vasudeva looked relieved as he bent down to see him. He had a gentle look on his face when he turned to Atisa.

'Do you think you know him?' The question came suddenly to Atisa, but it took the priest by surprise. His hands wavered, and then stilled. He stumbled over his answer, evasive in every way, 'He does look familiar…'

He turned to stare at Atisa and made up his mind, speaking up in a more resolute tone. 'He was here before. He is someone from Pataliputra, and this is where he came before to leave a message for me, a message I passed on in turn to be taken to someone he knows.' He clammed up then, stopped abruptly as if he really couldn't go on any more. 'I cannot tell you more. It is not for me to tell more.'

Atisa saw the agony of confusion on Vasudeva's face and almost felt sorry he had been prying. The priest didn't look a very secretive man, and so Atisa tried to lighten the atmosphere. Peering outside, he indicated, 'I do hope the trader is on time.' Vasudeva taking the cue, spoke up in a more jovial tone, 'The trader can help you, I am certain.' He stood up decisively, throwing his robe over one shoulder, 'Sometimes he dawdles, so maybe we could go to him instead.' He picked up a stick then, and Atisa saw it was one that had serrated edges. Vasudeva caught him smiling at it. 'You never know when one might need it. A priest too needs to do different things at times.'

He was still speaking as they trampled through the tall dry grass, pushing away withering old branches that stretched in their way.

'Ujjain is the nearest city to the north-west. There is Pataliputra to the south-east, Jhansi up north and the merchant city of Bharuch on the west, right by the sea. We seem to be in the very centre, in every way. Once the trader is here, you could reach there early morning. The trader often stops by here to visit the princess Prabhavati in the west. She is ruling in her husband's place, after the Sakas killed him. But the trader is not here today, and so things have gone awry.'

'Just a bit,' he added resolutely, but Atisa noticed that the anxious look was back on his face. Almost as if he was talking to himself, Vasudeva went on, 'But the Sakas will not stop him. Every man and group on the roads is familiar with him too. He can leave you at Ujjain, and it is the biggest city in these parts.' Atisa agreed. He wondered which route his mother had taken to escape. 'You know, there are all the tunnels, the hidden routes and the little-known maps that are part of the secret knowledge of the Sakas. Nurah the trader would know the right people to talk to.'

Atisa jumped out of his skin on hearing that name, 'Nurah… is that his name?'

Vasudeva in turn was startled by Atisa's reaction, 'Yes, why? Do you know him?'

Atisa couldn't quite bring himself to tell Vasudeva that he knew Nurah from his present, a present that was so different, so very far from the present the priest knew. This time it was the priest who smiled at Atisa's confusion, as if it mirrored his own of a few moments ago.

'Nurah knows the experts and the secret forest guides,' he said, suddenly becoming more eloquent. 'Even the pathfinders trust him.'

He stretched down low now, and it seemed he was sniffing out something. At last he stood up, looking satisfied, 'The pathfinders have marked out the path for us. See these small channels and the other tracks visible only in the moonlight…'

Excited, he set off at a steady pace, and Atisa carrying his folded-up flying machine found it hard to keep up. He couldn't follow most of Vasudeva's explanation either. 'There is a secret tunnel that leads to the other side of the mountains,' Vasudeva turned once to reveal. 'It is indeed very difficult to come here, unless they come like you,' said Vasudeva and grinned.

The Trader Reappears

They must have walked a long while before Vasudeva came to an abrupt halt. Atisa not too far behind saw his raised hand, almost like a warning. He heard the moving wind, the branches bending low and the low swish that overlay everything. Around him the world had flattened, and only later did he realize that the drumming sound he heard was that of horses galloping fast. It was the Sakas riding by once again. Their arrows flew like swishing crackers high in the sky, and one couldn't even hear a thing, for these were aimed so expertly. 'Lie low,' said Vasudeva, shinning up a tree as fast as he could. 'They must have sensed our presence,' he panted, but there was an element of doubt on his face. Atisa followed suit, climbing into a dense banyan tree. It was a grey morning, and a momentary thick black cloud covered him as the arrows slithered past. It was at that moment that his machine burst out of its restricting belt and ballooned up. Atisa was caught off guard, for moments unsure of what to do next. The wind was blowing strongly over the mountains and the balloon swelled up in no time, and it rose above the trees, bobbing teasingly over the soldiers. He climbed the branches as fast as he could, hoping he could pull the balloon in, or deflate it, before it sustained too much damage. Already he could see a gaping tear on it, something that would take him half a day to mend. But while the arrows flew all around, the horses did not venture near. He noticed then the uneven ledges of rock that led up the plateau, and the spray of the waterfall that rose like mist, high over everything. The rains of the nights before made its sounds more forceful. Assured by this, he reached for his machine cautiously, ducking in the thick branches, careful to keep out of sight. He could not fly away immediately either, but the machine had to be made less obtrusive. An open field was what he wanted most, to spread the whole thing out. To his relief, deflating the balloon proved easy. Atisa pressed a button, and with a sigh, a creak and a prolonged squeak, the balloon began folding up all over again. The shelves in the machine's small cockpit flattened themselves against the thin cloth walls, the seat folded up and then the cabin itself curled up in a ball. The balloon became an umbrella once again. Vasudeva looked sympathetic. 'Oh dear, that is most unexpected. Maybe the trader can take you to a place where it can be mended.'

By then, it was already morning and they had been walking for several hours. Vasudeva had stepped out several times, but there was still no sign of Nurah. 'Very well, we must then do something on our own,' the priest's words carried a grim resolution. His hands were shaking as he rummaged in the sack he carried. Vasudeva was indeed full of surprises. Now he produced a scroll and quickly unfolded it to reveal a map. He moved it this way and that, and as the silver light streamed down from the leaves overhead, Atisa saw that what looked grey and black had changed colour to reveal thin lines of blue and green. 'That is the way through the mountains, the tunnels and the waterfalls that can hide you.' He showed him where he had to start, a path hidden behind creepers that plunged down from the mountains. 'It is dark inside, and this tunnel is rarely frequented, but this is the only chance we have.'

Atisa nodded. He could see the mouth of the tunnel clearly now, and the priest watched him go, waving a last goodbye.

Once in the darkness inside, Atisa remembered the funny trader and his kite, the one he had inside his rucksack, wrapped closely with the decoder. He untied the kite from the folded-up balloon and in moments, it stretched like a rather long glow-worm and lit the way ahead for Atisa. The tunnel led deep inside and at the other end, after a long time, he saw Nurah waiting, atop an elephant, with a grin on his face. His hat rose high and tall over the trees giving away his presence. When Atisa's face appeared over the rocks that hid the entrance, Nurah's eyes widened in surprise. 'Well, well, fancy seeing you here.' 'I could say the same about you.' Nurah grinned, doffing his hat. 'Where are your yaks?' asked Atisa.

'Oh the yaks,' Nurah looked around as if he was indeed looking for them. 'I left them in the monastery around Peshawar. The grass is just right for them. Come on, hop on...'

Atisa looked dubiously at the elephant. 'I don't think...'

'There's nothing to it,' reassured Nurah, patting the one he sat on, 'He's the hardiest and the strongest.' Atisa saw for himself the elephant's magnificent tusks and its kind greying eyes. It let down its trunk to lift Atisa gently on to the howdah. He realized that he should have thanked Nurah for the kites, but Nurah appeared to be in a hurry to set off. 'The elephants will take us through the fastest routes, and we will reach Ujjain before nightfall.' They rode through dry thick forests and tall grass. The fallen leaves scrunched under the feet of the elephant herd, which in an orderly fashion, had fallen behind them. Atisa smelt the bittersweet smell of crushed leaves, the forest smell of clear water, animal presence and the unexpected fragrance of flowers. Nurah kept up a rambling conversation of his own. Atisa held on to his machine and tried to catch up on his sleep, falling over, every once in a while, on the cushions. 'Someone was supposed to have gone west to meet the princess, but he hasn't reached.' He pointed

anxiously towards the temple that now lay well and truly behind them, and Atisa knew for sure that all this – the injured man in the temple, the message for the princess and Nurah's own delay – was related in some manner. It was a puzzle that he was suddenly curious to unravel. 'There is an injured man back there... shouldn't we get help for him first?' Atisa asked. Nurah didn't look surprised as he heard that, and he quickly explained, 'I was waiting for a message from someone, and when he didn't come, I knew something was up...'

'Who is he?' asked Atisa, alert now, hoping to at least find out something. But it was Nurah's turn to be evasive now, and Atisa wondered why everyone was so secretive. Finally Nurah said in a slow hesitant voice, 'He is someone from the king's court. You know about the enmity with the Sakas, and so he had to travel secretly. But then he was attacked, which meant someone knew of his whereabouts...'

'He was a spy?'

'No, no.' Nurah looked shocked at that. 'No, he could never be that. But he's important, and we are glad he is safe. The princess would be very happy to know this.' Nurah looked thoughtful by the time he reached the end of his explanation. 'We need to make new plans because of what has happened.' He looked confused and drew with his hands in the air. 'You must come with me; it is quite a circuitous journey, I am afraid. I was actually headed to Jhansi at the other end...' Nurah looked at him expectantly and revealed that it was a very confidential mission he was headed for. He lowered his voice, 'But first I must go on to the west coast before I go to Jhansi. There is a trading party from Rome.' 'Going to Jhansi?' asked Atisa, 'isn't that a somewhat convoluted route if you are going west?'

Nurah shrugged and had a look of mock frustration on his face. 'What can you do? We go where the demand is.'

He sounded very officious and important, but the worry was back. 'In Ujjain, you must say you are a trader from across the eastern hills, which you are. They might ask you strange questions about that... tell them it's a magic umbrella. And after you get it repaired and I move on, you must meet this man. I am expecting him there, even if he hasn't reached yet. He might know things about your mother. He is one of the pathfinders.'

The pathfinders? And Atisa remembered the man who had led his mother to safety – men of a special tribe who moved in secret routes all on their own and knew the ways through the hidden dark paths between rocks and forest, behind the waterfalls and through the deep plateaus and mountains. But Nurah wouldn't say any more. He said he had to rush, and Atisa, clutching his folded-up machine and his rucksack, noticed in the fading light that he was poring over almost the same map he had seen with the priest. Was that also provided by the pathfinders?

The Lost Scrolls

By the time they rode into Ujjain, it had begun raining. Nurah told him more about the pathfinders. 'They are much in demand now. People are afraid of the eclipse, the rarest kind of eclipse ever. What if it all gets dark and stays that way? The only ones who can move through the dark are the pathfinders.'

The rain fell fast, and in slanting lines, striking their faces with some force. Tree branches duelled with each other, as if battling the wind. The temple bells had been chiming deliriously. Conch shells were being blown as if to ward away dangers if any, for Ujjain was a city of temples. The colony of the textile traders was at the western end of the city, and as Nurah went to register at the office of the Superintendent of Trade and Business, which was in the city centre, Atisa waited for the pathfinder. 'He will know where you are,' Nurah had said before leaving, in his all-knowing, yet mysterious way. But more than an hour later, no one had turned up. Meanwhile, in the crowds that milled around, a face repeatedly appeared amid the many others, a moustached turbaned man who leant on his staff and stared unabashedly, as if he was afraid to let Atisa out of his sight.

Finally by the time Nurah returned, the square was deserted, emptied of most of its occupants, even the man watching him had leant on his staff and gone to sleep. When Atisa pointed him out, Nurah didn't seem very perturbed or even look where he pointed. 'Oh, he's just one of those nomads. They are so used to living outdoors that nothing will make them feel comfortable inside.'

The textile trader who was to be their host greeted them warmly. He looked with great interest at Atisa's folded-up umbrella till Nurah revealed that it wasn't for sale. 'It's just something he carries around, because he is one of those long-distance travellers.' The textile trader, a bit disappointed at that, still persisted, 'Isn't that just too heavy for an ordinary umbrella?' 'It is indeed almost like a house when it's opened up,' said Nurah, and as if he realized that Atisa was uncomfortable with the attention, he smiled at the trader and said, 'This time I have the most fascinating stuff for you. Woollens from the high mountains, fancy robes from China and even fabrics that will make your house look even more magnificent.' 'All in good time, and I am not asking about that belt either,' laughed the trader. He insisted they rest first. 'Tomorrow, we will discuss all this.'

The servants too were greatly intrigued to see the huge umbrella, more so when Atisa gave his own specifications. 'It must be kept in the open, and since it's warm, I can sleep in the terrace.' 'Yes, indeed, that is a wonderful idea,' said the irrepressible Nurah, 'it can spread out like a bed, and has a very comfortable mattress.' Atisa would have glared at him, but just then one of the trader's assistants, unable to hold back his curiosity, asked him, 'Do you use it to ride on?' Since he spoke to him in the simple Prakrit that he understood, Atisa nodded, 'Yes, sometimes.'

As the servants bustled around them, filling up jars of water, spreading mattresses and lighting incense sticks that spread an instant fragrance, a sudden storm came up. It did not give any advance warning; instead the windows and doors slammed shut as the wind came racing down the streets, carrying pillars of dust, and the tolling of the temple bells changed to a great clamour. 'It's common in these parts and won't upset your plans in the least,' said the imperturbable Nurah, 'just duck, cover your face, for they bring in stone and grit from the desert in the west.' Nurah's words were muffled because he was doing precisely that. And the cloth over his face fluttered and shook, as the dust greased into it. There was grit in Atisa's mouth as well, and the storm whooshed and rushed past things, in no definite direction, and it was quite a few moments before it all stilled. And yet Nurah did not raise his head, mumbling instead through his covered face, 'Sometimes the lull is deceptive.' But this time the dust storm did not return.

Nurah got up a long while later, dusted himself casually and the servants returned as well. They brought the room to a semblance of normalcy in a matter of moments. It did seem as if they were used to it.

It was evening, and Atisa went out with Nurah into the bazaars. He now had to meet the officials who would give him the permit to move westwards. 'Everything does seem to be very bureaucratic,' Atisa said to himself. Nurah put away his ear trumpet, which had caught Atisa's soft whisper, and proceeded to explain, 'It is necessary, for Ujjain is close to the frontline, or what was the frontline some years ago, when the king waged war against the Sakas. And there is the eclipse...' Then in very even tones so as to give nothing away, he said, 'You realize we are being followed, don't you?' And slowly and very deliberately, he jerked to where a cloaked man stood, hidden in the crowd, and Atisa knew instantly it was the same man who had been watching him earlier.

Lanterns were strung up by the sidewalks now, and vendors had spread their wares. They shouted out their offerings, hoping to shout their rivals down. Atisa noted the fragrant oils and perfumes, the painted clay toys, fruits, cloth garments and strange aphrodisiacs, which, according to the vendors, could cure the most incurable of ailments. As they stood wondering what to do next, someone approached them. Atisa saw his face in the light of the lanterns, a man with a patch on one eye and broken teeth. 'Are you trying to sell us broken teeth?' asked Nurah, and Atisa thought that was very rude of him. But the man said in a wheedling, whining tone, 'There are some scrolls in my possession. I have reasons to believe that they are very valuable.'

He lowered his voice, watching them both carefully, as if he would run the moment an alarm was raised, 'They are about the eclipse.' He whispered. He had to be careful because his teeth whistled, chattered and clattered, providing a rhythm to all that he said. 'The precautions one must take, and the probability that it will happen, the scrolls say it all,' said the man, who simply refused to give up.

Nurah seemed impatient, and he was eager to be on his way. 'They were passed on to me,' wheedled the man. 'Wait!' said Atisa. Hearing this, Nurah stopped. The man looked at him in gratitude before he explained in a rush, for he knew Nurah would still try and stop him, 'The man who gave them to me said that they were of no use. But I have some knowledge of these things. I was a student of Varahamihira.'

'That is indeed the name,' said Nurah, clapping his head, 'that is the name of the astronomer I keep forgetting.' 'But where did you find these scrolls?' stepped in Atisa. 'Someone with wings, who came running through these forests, gave them to me. He said that they were of no use to him. He had been tricked into taking them when he wanted something else.' Atisa stared at the man, his heart almost stopping as he mentioned the man with wings. It could be the same man who had chased his mother some days ago. Nurah next to him had gone so very still that Atisa knew he had to be hiding something. Finally, a long time later, Nurah sighed heavily, held out his hand and said, 'Really, let me see...'

He held up the scrolls and looked at them, squinting his eyes. Atisa peered too and saw complex diagrams, an angry-looking sun, a cringing moon, an obeisant earth and Mars, as a skulking figure far away. It was in all a human portrayal of what the eclipse was about. 'Why...,' Nurah let out a cry of excitement before he clapped a hand over his mouth. Then he wouldn't say any more.

'Can I have this? Who gave it to you?' asked Atisa, knowing this could help him understand various things, such as who had attacked the injured man as he had run through the forests. Just what had the man on wings been after, if he hadn't wanted these scrolls after all?

The man had a frightened look now. But he nodded, almost in reply to Atisa's scattered thoughts and all his unasked questions. He looked all over his shoulder and then said, 'He was on wings, said it wasn't any of my business to know. But I was curious. And he had a thin moustache, a narrow, pointed face and a strange way of walking on his toes, as if he had been on those wings for a long time. "Take this," he told me, "I was fooled. Fooled." And his scream was like a thousand vultures crying or several hundred vampires dancing in a cemetery.' Even Nurah shuddered at that description. It took a long time for the shudders to die away. 'So that is our man,' he said, 'at least we now know who he was.' He stopped, and then took off his hat and blew his trumpet. It was something he always did when he had made up his mind. He looked relieved, almost happy. 'Indeed,' said the man. And his teeth wobbled and chattered, and the word scattered itself. 'We have to look out for him,' Nurah said in as expressionless a voice as possible.

Atisa looked lost; he had to make Nurah explain some things to him. Why did he look so relieved when it was this same man who had followed his mother? He must indeed be dangerous if he could so grievously harm the man, now injured, in the priest's temple. 'Can I have that umbrella then?' said the man with the scrolls. It seemed Nurah hadn't heard, for he went on, almost in an undertone. 'We know who he is, and we must stop him too.' He said it in a low tone, and Atisa knew he was referring to the man with wings. He saw Nurah looking at him and then quickly look away. There was a warning look there, but Atisa couldn't be sure, for the next moment he had turned to the man with the broken teeth, gently dissuading him. 'You should, if you happen to travel to Pataliputra, seek an appointment with the great physician Dhanvantri. He can fix your teeth.'

'Give me new ones?' said the other man, the wind catching in his throat and making him whistle. 'Yes, and if you should come across this man again, you must let us know.'

'Yes, but I don't think he ever left the forests. He said he had to find someone and he wasn't ever going back to Pataliputra without him.' Nurah now looked really worried. 'It is true then,' he said. 'There is still great danger, and the princess Prabhavati must be told.' Then he relented, when he saw the confusion in Atisa's eyes. 'There is an important noble from the king's court who set off for Bharuch on the west coast. We were surprised and also alarmed, because all astrologers had advised against travel. He said it was urgent, and then he didn't return. We thought it was the Sakas who had something to do with this, but this description... is of someone else, someone infinitely more dangerous. We fear he may harm him again and the Sakas blamed unfairly. The princess must be told and if possible, we may have to request her to move to Pataliputra.' He shook his head, forced a smile on his face and said, 'We must find out, simply find out before he can do more harm.'

When they returned, they found that the pathfinder, who

was to take Atisa farther westwards, had still not turned up. 'Dina, he's never late. He must have been held up,' consoled Nurah, knowing Atisa was in a hurry to move on. The night fell quickly as it did in the interior lands, and there was a cool breeze. Their beds were placed outside on the terrace, and it was when he was sleeping in the courtyard that the man stepped in. The balloon moved in the breeze, its folds rising and falling. Atisa wouldn't have heard him but for the sound catcher, which picked up the soft creeping of footsteps, the patter, the rushed breathing of someone advancing slowly, and he was awake in no time. First he saw a shadow appear over the walls, but this was not a fearful one. Whoever it was, seemed to be advancing very cautiously forward.

'I am Dina, the pathfinder,' the man said, a watchful look in his eyes. He looked at Atisa, and a strange look passed his eyes. 'It was your mother whom I led through the mountains.'

Nurah rose too, pulling his ear trumpet out and saying with some annoyance, 'Bother you Dina, even your whisper makes my ear scratch.' Then they exchanged looks of mischief, and Nurah shrugged, 'So I can see you've met.' 'I am glad I met you, and yes it was your mother who saved the...'

Dina must have exchanged looks again with Nurah, because he stopped and his expression turned grave. 'I am here, and very late too, because I must warn you... the danger is not yet over. And even I am a suspect.'

Nurah lifted his hands, but Dina stopped him, 'No, I know. I and those like me are still seen with suspicion. We are seen as the Sakas' allies. And our friend, who your mother helped, is still in danger...'

He looked at the two of them before going on, 'and so are you... For the man will stop at nothing, now that his identity has been compromised. He knows that you know.'

He broke off, shrugging. 'I wish I could tell you more, but

we have to be very careful. Then it is also the time of the eclipse. You are strangers in the city, and with a strange object like that umbrella, you are noticeable. People will be suspicious, even hostile. The eclipse is causing some unease.' 'Yes, I didn't know it was so bad, now that you tell me that the threat is still there,' said Nurah. He looked at Atisa apologetically as if to say that everything would be explained in good time. Dina leant forward, and Nurah drawing Atisa in told them of the new plans that were now necessary. 'The great astronomer in Jhansi has to set off for Pataliputra immediately. Too much has already happened, and we cannot risk anymore.' Atisa had never seen Nurah look more decisive. 'And he doesn't want this nonsense. Somehow, we have to make sure his papers reach him.'

Nurah was thinking fast, and so his words vanished in places as his thoughts raced on ahead.

'At Jhansi, there is his daughter, we must tell her that Varahamihi…'

And once more, Nurah had forgotten the name.

Varahamihira, this time it was Atisa who prompted.

And Nurah clapped his head, 'Of course that is the name. I have finally remembered it. Tell him his papers have been found.' The pathfinder grinned. He seemed all too familiar with Nurah's forgetfulness. 'No wonder, you found it difficult to get a meeting with him, when you passed Jhansi the last time…' 'Yes,' Nurah looked abashed, 'He is still annoyed with me, though I knew the ships would come to Bharuch, and I promised to get some important equipment for him. But then things went wrong…' Nurah shook his head, then turned to Atisa almost with a pleading look on his face. 'Will you go on ahead, to Jhansi, on your machine? Return the scrolls to the great astronomer and persuade him to set off for the capital and convince the emperor, and I will soon meet you.'

Atisa gasped. All this meant a total change of plans. He had thought he would set off with Dina to find his mother, but Nurah's plans meant a change in direction. 'You must. The empire's well-being depends on this. Heaven knows the superstitions and rumours the eclipse is fuelling. You go to Jhansi and convince Lilavati, his very clever daughter. She is the only one who can persuade her father, make him travel to Pataliputra in time for the great eclipse.' Atisa looked disheartened, and Dina hastened to console him. 'It will be all right. If the person we think is the real villain, then your mother is safe, because she has headed north-west. In the meantime, we need your help desperately.'

'Your flying machine would be especially invaluable,' Nurah said, pointing to the umbrella leaning against a corner. 'There is no one who can fly as fast as you can and in these times, we need you. No one will know, but this kingdom will owe its future to you.'

Dina laughed ruefully seeing the confusion on Atisa's face and how very lost he was, 'He is a salesman and used to making such speeches, but I know him, especially when he says things in such a heartfelt manner. It would really help us.' He looked earnestly at Atisa. 'I assure you, your mother is safe.' Dina nodded and turned to Nurah, but he was already gathering up his goods. He had to get these weighed and examined. With his sacks and holders around him, he suddenly looked like a giant tortoise on the move. And his hat had risen higher so that it rose above the sacks, and Atisa saw the bell now.

'That's a warning for people to keep people away,' grinned Nurah as he said goodbye, promising they would meet again soon. Dina, scanning the skies, said there was every chance it would rain soon, and he offered to wait with Atisa till the skies cleared.

The Unexpected Happens

Dina the pathfinder's predictions turned out to be accurate. The very next day it began raining, and in a matter of a few hours it had picked up. From a soft drizzle, it soon rose to become a steady, unrelenting downpour. Their host, the trader, looked up, scanned the skies and agreed it hadn't rained like this ever. 'It's bad for business and for everything else,' he said grimly. The servants rushed in, pulling in the dyed cloth sheets that had been hung out to dry. These had been spread out on the courtyard that overlooked the riverbank, but the rain came down so hard that on some sheets the colours had already run, and the river now ran purple and red. An hour later, with the rain like an unending grey curtain outside, the roads turned into rivers, and men ventured out in boats shaped like baskets. They looked like hooded figures in grey, silhouetted in a misty curtain. Atisa knew this was no time or place to rev up the machine and fly away. It was then that the textile trader turned up with horses, two stallions that stood almost docile, with heads lowered, stomping their feet, despite the rain. He was evasive as to where he had got them from. 'They are expert workhorses and will help you ford the waters.' Dina whispered once they were off, 'He must have got them from the Sakas, who else? Now that they are retreating, they are all selling off their fine horses.' He reached forward and patted the horse nearest him, 'This is the finest Arabian one you will ever ride.' They splashed high across knee-deep puddles that had appeared in the streets; in places these rose like small fountains. Then as they took the uneven mountain road, the horses were more sure-footed and even graceful.

As they rode on, the rain slowed to a steady drizzle. They were passing an area where low grey hills and rough, rocky patches appeared, with straggly trees in between. There were miles and miles of dry scrubland, and no one else but the two of them. But all this soon proved deceptive, for unexpectedly, something moved in the rocks, and as the horses shied away as rocks came bounding down, a black shadow fell over the road as well. *Bandits!* Dina taken off guard could only screech the word, his voice breaking off at the end. The ambush happened most unexpectedly. There had been no noise, except that Atisa did notice the sudden dip in the rocks and the way a lone branch moved when there was no wind. Then there was the darkness, the advancing brown cloud of dust, as the men with half their faces covered in black cloth thundered in with their horses, and they had been encircled in no time. They pointed spears and with rough gestures asked them to follow. *Make your horses ride in through that valley. Stay behind us, and take no wrong step.* As they rode side by side, Dina picked a moment to whisper to Atisa, 'Talk of the devil. They are the Sakas. They are reduced to nomadic horsemen, some of whom are renegade soldiers.'

Atisa, upset by what had happened, could only nod in response, 'This does upset all our plans.'

The men led them to their chief, who had long straggly hair that he kept brushing away from his face. Every time he did so, he revealed a craggy face full of scars. He looked at the two of them with great interest and pointed to Atisa's rolled-up machine. 'My men said there was a big merchant spotted with his umbrella and a real fancy belt. And we got you, a merchant and a magician.' He grinned, rubbing his hands in glee, but

Atisa noticed a certain wariness too. Like most people, he was cautious about the umbrella and the belt and wouldn't do much to anger him. Atisa grinned back insouciantly at that thought, and the bandit chief ordered his men to move on.

The night was setting in, and they had to set up camp in a much safer place, higher up in the hills. When they finally stopped a long while later, they were by a clearing near a small pond in the forest. As some of the bandits busied themselves making a fire, and skinning an antelope, the others surrounded them. They looked ready for some banter and trivial conversation. The flying machine with its look of an oversized, giant umbrella seemed to be the focus of all attention. 'We are all indeed curious about it. It seems something special in your country for you do not seem to move without it.' Atisa warned them not to touch his machine. 'You will be cursed, the heavens will fall on you and your descendants will never see the light of day. Only my family knows the secrets of the giant umbrella.'

But the men laughed, good-naturedly. 'Oh we have ways of making you talk,' said one of them with considerable dark humour, but Atisa noticed that they skirted around the machine carefully, making no attempt to touch it or even glance at it. They weren't treated too badly though, except that they were kept tightly bound and gagged most of the time. The few times their hands were unbound, he noticed Dina bending and picking up a few stones and pebbles that he simply dropped inside a small bag tied to his waist. He wouldn't let on why he was doing this. The bandit leader apologized to Atisa as he trussed him up again. 'We know you are not going to escape, but we don't quite trust your friend here.' He rolled his eyes, laughing, as Dina pursed his lips in anger. 'We know too well the pathfinders.'

A day later, they heard the sound of an elephant, and then someone dark and burly with a thick moustache draped over his ears in a ceremonial fashion came to inspect them. From the whispers and hurried snatches of conversation around him, Atisa realized that this was a slave trader. He walked ponderously, as if with each step he wanted to register his presence on the earth. Two attendants followed him, holding an umbrella over his head. This was too small for him, however, and the attendants struggled to keep up. If they dawdled or the umbrella moved away, he turned around to whip them with no warning, even as he carried on a conversation with the bandit chief. The bandit chief smiled ingratiatingly at Atisa and said, 'This one is some foreigner, long hair and young as well. His umbrella, which only he can touch, has magic. There's a secret charm in his belt, but it blinks a warning if you go too near. I do think he can have his uses though.' They stopped where Dina was and looked more dubiously at him.

'This one hunts and forages, so I don't know what use he could be in a city, but...'

Beside him, Atisa felt the pathfinder stiffen in indignation.

'Can he handle horses?'

'Yes, I think he could,' said the chief, 'though we did have to escort them through the forest.' The pathfinder quivered with noticeable rage; the bandit chief grinned at his discomfiture while the slave trader twirled his moustache. He nodded once, the chief bowed and so a deal was struck.

As they travelled to the west, the slave trader was carried on his palanquin by his attendants, and Dina and Atisa rode alongside on horses. Atisa's faithful umbrella was fixed to his saddle. The forests were thick around them, interspersed by low rounded hills, and Atisa longed for some open space that would allow his machine to open up and help them escape. The slave trader lay back on the cushions, twirling his moustache in delight as he looked at the two of them on either side of his palanquin. 'This time I am sure I have struck a good deal. The

Roman traders will pay me in gold.' 'You will perform before the Roman nobles,' he murmured, looking at Atisa and the umbrella that bobbed and jigged every time they rode over a rough patch, and Atisa held on to it frantically. The trader tapped his rings and again murmured, 'Oh my, they do like these fancy things.'

He told them tales of the Roman ships and traders, and how he had once seen a secret performance of gladiators battling lions. 'It's all banned you know, but in the island of Corinth, it is still held secretly. And I picked up a lion from here.'

He had their attention and laughed. 'And we had to feed the animal tons and tons of fish. There was a huge shark too, and then there were sharks chasing us all the way across the seas, seeking revenge. Oh, but we were indeed glad to get away.' A frightened bearer missed his step and stepped on a boulder, which then fell several feet below. Clouds of dust rose, turning everything black and smoky, and only the horses stood still.

'You can see how amazingly well trained my horses are, infinitely better than my servants,' said the trader unctuously once they had stopped sneezing.

Two days later, when they reached Bharuch on the west, where the air itself was dry and salty, the trader managed to slip his way through into the city. Atisa noticed the coins that changed hands with the guards at the gate. The trader did seem to be well connected; he did not need the usual permits and passes that regulated movement into a city. But Bharuch in the west had only recently been in the frontline of war. The Sakas had been defeated, but the threat remained. The weather here was drier, and it seemed the rain had never happened. A hot, blustery wind had started blowing. They raised their cloaks well over their heads, and because everyone was doing it, they did not draw attention.

After a day at an inn, the trader rowed them towards a big ship. It was sleek and long and had the square boxed sails common to big ships that sailed the vast oceans of the world. There were armed soldiers all round, with their helmets and short vests of armour. They passed columns of soldiers and sullen-faced rowers, before they were taken below to the hold, where they were made to wait again.

The Roman trader was at his bath, and Atisa realized that some things never changed. People in positions of power still made you wait. The pathfinder leant against the wall and caught up on his sleep, and Atisa played chess with himself on the deck floor, before he found someone at the far end of the hall playing a game of darts all on his own, aiming at a small board hung up on the wall. The other man tossed a few darts to Atisa. After some of Atisa's throws had gone off the mark, the man told him that he was an archer. 'That's why my aim is better,' he said, noting Atisa's rueful face, and then something made him reveal more. His voice lowered and he cautiously said, 'I am one of the Sakas,' and then there was a meaningful silence. 'But I got tired of the senseless small battles. I wanted to fight the big battles, where one would travel far and encounter strange new worlds and real dangers. I was indebted to this trader for I thought he was doing me a big favour, but he sent me on a heinous mission. He was bribed by the Saka tribes, and I was part of the assassination mission that led to the killing of King Rudrasena, the son-in-law of the great king Vikramaditya, a crime that was never solved. And since then, I have been disenchanted, even with my own self.' Atisa listened to him stunned. The man looked abjectly remorseful, and for once Atisa was at a loss for words. 'I came to know only later who I had killed. I was asked to aim at a man sitting on an elephant, in a howdah, as he waited for the lions. It was pride in my skill that led to this crime. And now I'd do anything to put that right, to put my talents to some use.' He looked at Atisa and beyond him at Dina, who was still sleeping, his mouth open.

His ears twitched as if he was, even while sleeping, alert to the slightest sound. He lowered his voice, and looking away, so as not to arouse suspicion, said, 'Maybe I can help you escape. There is always a right time.'

But at Bharuch, no time seemed to be right. A sullen heat had settled in, the wind had died down completely, and it seemed the weather would see little change for a while. There were sailing ships that had been anchored for days. People said it was the eclipse that was making the weather behave strangely. There was an edginess to everything. The soldiers snapped and snarled for no reason, and Atisa and Dina were careful to stay away from them. The rowers waited on deck in a sullen silence. The slave trader was as full of menace as he was unctuous. There was little hope of escaping, for they were watched over by his men, who cracked the whip at the slightest excuse. Sometimes they laughed as they played with the spears, aiming at things they tossed above; even the birds were not spared. The gulls and storks had made a pretty picture, the shades of white and grey in their wings juxtaposed against the endless blue of the skies. But now the raucous laughter of the sailors made Atisa wince, and he was in tears at the way they took the gulls. The piercing screams and the terrified flapping of wings, as the birds struck by arrows fell to their deaths in the sea, filled the sky. The wait seemed interminable, for on the ship there was nothing much to do, and as astrologers appeared in the port and read out the latest forecasts, Atisa knew a week or more had gone by. The astrologers sat in their tents not too far away on shore, each one determined to prove his skills over the other. Yet even they feared making a definite pronouncement: no one would say if it was safe enough to sail. They would look at their scrolls and say it was best to wait. Atisa remembered the lost scrolls he still carried with him, and when he had some time to himself, he tried to decipher what they said. It made everyone, especially the soldiers, laugh. *This slave thinks he is a scholar.* They pointed him out to the others and laughed even more. Atisa blinked away his tears.

The eagle-eyed watch had slackened over the days as nothing happened. They could now walk around on the deck, freed of their manacles, and they noticed the bigger ships and smaller boats standing absolutely still around them. Nothing seemed to move; there was not even the slightest flutter in the sails. As a quiet fell around, the strange fluttering noise that had been muted before, now made itself more apparent. There did seem to be an unusual creature making a racket below. 'We are taking an entire aviary for the Roman nobles,' said the trader, grinning. 'Such beautiful birds, and they can make so much noise. You'd think things of beauty would all have sweet, dulcet voices.' He scratched his ears, wiped the sweat from his forehead and laughed raucously, 'But the prettier they are, the uglier they sound.'

Sometimes the trader could be in a far more difficult mood. He would bark orders at random, and one day when the noise below got too much, he had the bird trainer brought to him. The man who stood before him was like a small bird himself. His hands nervously fluttered as he bowed before the trader, and his arms and shoulders shrugged and moved as the birds, which followed him everywhere, now settled themselves all over him. They trusted him, and he was the best perch they found. The parakeets and the swallows flew high up, and some dropped down in an ungainly manner, while others returned to the safety of the man's shoulders. The trader cracked his whip, and the birds shrieked in unison. 'Can you not keep these creatures in control?'

'How can I, my master?' the birdman wailed, 'these birds, used to the blue skies and the freedom and the wind in their wings, are miserable cooped up below.' 'And it smells,' said the trader, cracking his whip once more. 'It does smell, my master. It could make them fall sick and die.' The motions the trader was making with his whip died away, and he looked up sharply, suspecting the man of impertinence. 'Really and truly, my master. They need their time in the open. See, aren't they happier seeing the blue skies around them? I implore you, my master, please let them be here for a while.'

The trader looked bored with it all by now. He tossed his whip away, wiped his forehead and said, 'very well, but no noise, remember no noise. And no smart tricks either, or else these birds will make a wonderful meal.' The bird trainer nodded abjectly, folding his hands in gratitude. Only Atisa saw the surreptitious wink passed between the birdman and the pathfinder.

Another day passed by, listless and unmoving like the ones before. Atisa had no appetite and lay in the shade, his balloon spread out like a mattress under him. It was with a sense of mounting excitement that he realized that some of the calculations in the scrolls were making sense to him. These were papers of the great astronomer Varahamihira and were based on all the work done by his forefathers, who were great astronomers themselves. Based on the old wisdom and his own gathered knowledge, the astronomer had calculated that the eclipse was less than ten days away, but to relate it to strange weather phenomena was unscientific. Atisa found himself fascinated by what he was reading.

It's warm because such spells do happen once in a while. Our rulers must simply learn to prepare for the future, and if they are just rulers, they will spend on silos and warehouses to store grain and reservoirs to contain water, and lessen the taxes. Atisa put the papers down, and the papers did not move or even flutter away. It was that kind of a hot, dry day, and everything was still, especially in the afternoon. He yawned,

and beside him, Dina stretched and then looking at nothing in particular said, 'We have made a plan to escape.' The stones inside his robe jingled, and not for the first time, Atisa wondered why he had been collecting them. 'They aren't all stones,' Dina grinned and then quickly looking around, caught the eye of the birdman. He scratched his earring almost as if it were a signal of some kind, and the birdman nodded, looking around quickly. *Now watch. And be ready.* Atisa looked puzzled. 'We had to plan this to escape. Once the birds go crazy, jump down to the other side where there is a boat waiting.' Dina pulled out a catapult and with quick sharp movements aimed peas and smaller pebbles at the sky. They were so tiny as to be invisible, and for those initial moments, no one noticed Dina's movements as he used his catapult leaning against the wall, in the shadows.

The birds were surprised at first, then lost momentum and began flying blindly. The birdman hid in the shadows, and the birds looked for him. They made a huge cloud, they swooped and flew high, in circles, and different bird noises filled the air, their calling mingling with their wildly fluttering wings and their falling feathers – parakeets, pelicans, herons, storks, egrets, all flying in unison, in no fixed direction, their cries loud and erratic, and hard to bear in that golden afternoon. *Come quickly.* Dina the pathfinder took his hand, and they ducked and swooped through the dense cloud, for the panic and confusion had drawn in other birds from the shore too. Gulls and storks scattered in alarm, making the waves lap higher than before, and the world turned blurry around them.

Behind them, Atisa heard the patter and the jingle of anklets and knew the birdman was following them too. *We have to get away. Fast.* Atisa was quick to scramble down the rope, his machine secure on his back. The rope bobbed and swung often, so his feet came up against the ship's wooden walls. It was with some relief that his feet chanced on the boat. The birdman was the last, and as Dina picked up the oars, he motioned to Atisa to begin rowing too. He said that the birds would follow. Atisa bent, stretching hard at the oars, eager to get away. He wished his flying machine could become a broomstick and make their getaway that much easier. He hardly dared to look back and when he did, the slave trader and his soldiers were dark, menacing forms straining over the deck. 'Don't be afraid,' said Dina, 'they will not raise an alarm.' 'That is because smuggling, especially of captured men as slaves, is forbidden. He could be banned forever, and trade with Rome could come to an end. He would not take that risk by following us.'

As they neared the port, a short distance away, Dina looked worried, 'The authorities could create a fuss,' he said, looking at Atisa's folded-up machine, 'and we don't even have the money to bribe them.'

It was just as he had said. As they neared, a port official sailed up in his white boat and peered over, his voice rasping with suspicion, 'and just what is that equipment?' 'It is a tent and a bedroll,' said Atisa smoothly. The man nodded, looked away as if he was convinced by his reply and then nodded again. 'We still have to be careful. It is the time of the eclipse, and many people are trying to cause evil. We have to be certain.' He looked out at the sea, at the ships and then back again at them, but he was looking at nothing in particular. 'That does look very suspicious,' he said, looking nonchalant, but Atisa wasn't fooled. 'I cannot open it unless I find an open field or the open sea.' 'Be my guest,' the official grinned, indicating the wide sea.

Atisa rowed hard, found a space that stretched between boats like a vast blue field and made the folded-up machine stand up, as carefully as he could, for the boat jigged and bounced in the waves. It looked like a tall, folded-up mast.

He began pushing the bellows, and the machine stretched out, creakily and very unmusically. The balloon blew up slowly, taking its time, and far away the officers watched as did those on the anchored ships, some near and others far away, looking like small cardboard objects. The kites fluttered and stretched into shape. The cabin yawned and expanded, and then rose slowly up, and as the balloon took up more space, stretching out on the boat, they were pushed to its very margins.

'When I say now, you have to jump on to the cabin,' Atisa told Dina. And that is just what the pathfinder did. He leapt into the cabin so very quickly that it bounced and shook and rattled with unexpected force. In moments, they were up and away, leaning below to say goodbye to the birdman, who now had the birds and the boat entirely to himself. In delight, the birds settled down all around him and playfully flew around the boat, and the birdman waved at them as he rowed calmly and happily towards the shore. 'Fly straight over the port and the city and back into the forests,' said Dina. 'But Nurah...,' said Atisa.

'Don't worry, we will catch up with Nurah...' Atisa looked back towards the sea, now much farther away. They flew over Bharuch with its low houses, narrow streets and crowded markets. He realized that too many days had already gone by. 'Nothing is ever wasted, my friend,' consoled Dina as if he read his mind. 'We rescued the birdman. You learnt things about the eclipse, and then we do know about the smugglers. Believe me, they will lie low for a while now.'

Atisa smiled in contrition, and as they sailed in the sky that refused to relent, the pathfinder complained about how unusually hot it all was. 'In my time, they call it global warming,' said Atisa. Dina looked puzzled, and Atisa settled down for a much-needed snooze.

The Escape

The sea was far behind in no time, its waves a faint roar, unending and constant, when the pathfinder reiterated with urgency, 'We must go and return the scrolls to the great astronomer. He will be very happy to get them back.' Atisa couldn't help but be annoyed at this. The plans kept changing all the while. When would he ever go in search of his mother? He looked at his map checker and found that the temple where he had met Vasudeva was right on the way, just at the halfway point to Jhansi. 'It will all end well,' said Dina almost in consolation, 'when this adventure of our lifetime is over, as 'it will be.' Somehow, the way he said that made Atisa feel very strange.

It took them almost the entire day before they found themselves in the forests again, and it seemed time had stood still, for like before, there was the priest waiting. There was no reason for him to do that, for neither Atisa nor Dina had plans to stop by, but it was Dina's way of leaning forward a bit too anxiously, long before the machine touched down on the land, that warned Atisa. Something was wrong; it was evident in the way the lantern in the priest's hand flickered and wavered. It was as if the man holding it had been doing so for too long, and his hands were trembling and just about to give up on him. He could see no horses around or even any sign of the warriors. Perhaps everyone was afraid of the eclipse and was lying low. That thought considerably relieved Atisa, and he descended like before on the plateau. He skidded over the grey stones of the plateau, skated over the trees and he saw the kites affix themselves to the trees, and so the machine came to a halt, balanced on trees. The kites fluttered and moved, but the flying machine was now perfectly still.

'It's the eclipse, now not too far away,' said Dina, only a bit relieved. 'It makes the soldiers afraid too; for many, it means the end of the world.' Pulling in the balloon, Atisa folded it up in the umbrella before rushing quickly down. He was glad that the noise made by the boulder he dislodged was drowned in the noise of the waterfall. It took on a thunderous force on his sound catcher. It was the sound catcher that alerted him. He heard the rustling of the bushes and the crackle of pebbles skittering, and it made Dina draw out his sword. Dina took the cloth off his mouth, which had muffled his voice, and with his raised hand motioned Atisa to be careful. He had heard the crackle of a twig and had seen in front, the erratic movement of the lantern.

The priest stepped forward, and Atisa gasped, 'He has been injured.' The priest held his injured wrist in one hand and then snuffed out the lantern before dropping it. Unable to speak, the priest sat down on the ground with his head in his hands.

In that silence, there was only the sound of his terrible breathing. Then he looked up and explained in faltering tones. 'That man came, the one who had chased him before. He had a wild look on his face and I fought him. I was not a moment too late. But in the melee...,' he broke down again, coughed and couldn't complete. It was Dina who whispered hoarsely, 'Where is he?'

He stopped, looked at Atisa and added with some hesitation, 'Where did your patient go?'

The priest shook his head, motioned with his hand and said, 'Just disappeared. Our man just ran into the forest.' He was weeping now, 'And I thought he was recovering so well once Nurah was here with the special medicines from the princess.' Atisa, despite his alarm, was taken aback on hearing that. 'Nurah was back here. Well, he does seem to have gotten here very fast. How did I miss him?'

Dina bent down and patted Vasudeva on the shoulders. 'It really isn't your fault, Vasudeva.' He looked up and saw Atisa's puzzled face, then hesitated before explaining to Atisa, 'You must know, Nurah is on a top-secret mission.' He helped Atisa stow away his folded-up machine in a nook on a tree, and once it was covered by dry branches, it drew no one's attention. The priest went on, rubbing his hands after it was all done, 'Nurah dropped by to leave some medicines, those sent specially by the princess Prabhavati, who he was taking to safety. These had a miraculous effect on our friend, who was ill for so long. But the man still came, he will never give up the chase…'

Atisa though was still thinking about Nurah and that it was very strange that he had missed him. Vasudeva's explanation left him even more puzzled. So the injured man had to be someone important. The princess had ensured that the medicines reached him, and Nurah must have travelled fast to reach the forests so very quickly, though Atisa himself had been held up. And everyone it seemed, especially Dina and the priest, was prepared to protect him at all costs, not even willing to identify him. But the priest, who had recovered somewhat, was walking on ahead, stopping once in a while to talk to them over his shoulder.

The forest was dry and leaves scrounged under his feet, and if he didn't look, the sharp pebbles could hurt. And then the contour of the forest changed too. Once they had climbed a hill, they descended into the forest's thickness all over again, and he couldn't let the priest out of his sight, as he made his way turning this way and that, moving into a sudden copse of trees and emerging just as quickly through it. The priest broke into a run as the grey contours of the temple came into view among the trees. But his steps stilled as he neared. Atisa assumed he did not want to disturb the man who was still recovering in the temple's inner room.

They heard the soft patter of water falling somewhere, the wind in the temple bells, a squirrel's impatient foraging in the trees and nothing else. But because the stillness stretched and nothing seemed to break it, Atisa knew within a few moments that something was wrong. The priest stood rigid; he did not turn around even once, his hands holding on to the stone wall as if he was trying hard from screaming out loud. There were tears running down his cheeks. It made Dina rush forward and hold him by the shoulders. He did not have to say it, but it was clear something was wrong. The room inside was heavy with smoke that changed colour, turning blue and then grey, and as it surged forward, he saw shiny beads embedded in it. It was Dina who grabbed him by the shoulder in warning. The priest had already covered his face and was running away. Atisa saw the rough tears in the priest's eyes, the scratchy, wrinkled look on his face, before he let himself be led away. It had to be poison gas of some kind.

Run away fast, Dina shouted a warning behind, and a long time later the three of them reached a clearing of some kind. On the plateau, where a stream flowed quite near, they rested on some rocks amid a copse of trees, watching some peacocks fly hurriedly away as they rushed up. Vasudeva tried to speak, but no words came. They knew some evil had happened, that the man in Vasudeva's care was no longer there and there was only that terrible poisonous smoke. 'He will stop at nothing now,' said Dina grimly. 'That poison means he is armed and well equipped. Even a small dose can kill.' 'He has been here, look,' Vasudeva spoke now in a voice bereft of all meaning. He pointed, and Atisa immediately recognized the rough cotton quilt from the temple. He had seen the sick man wrapped up in it only some days ago. The quilt now lay forlorn and discarded, by one of the rocks, in a quiet corner. 'The fact that it's all folded up, not scattered, means he did not drop it in a rush. He must be around,' said Atisa. The priest appeared not to have heard him. He leant against the wall and went on, low and almost in a whisper as if his strength was ebbing out. 'He had a wild look about him… he had to have his prey. I do not understand how he had come to know. As for myself, I only knew what his intentions were the moment he entered the cave that led to the temple.'

Vasudeva drank water thirstily from the leaf that Dina held out for him before going on. 'He looked delirious. He must have chased him for days and nights altogether because he didn't seem to be himself. I have never seen someone look so mad. He engaged me in a swordfight, though I am not the best swordsman ever.' He paused, perhaps wondering at his own immodesty, and gingerly touched his injured wrist, which Dina had now wrapped up with cloth torn away from the quilt. 'But in his feverish, mad state, he fought hard, as if the demons were in him.' 'You did indeed fight well and hard,' said Dina, 'The princess would be happy to know this.'

Vasudeva looked even more miserable, 'It doesn't matter, not if…' 'So who is he? You have to let me know,' Atisa insisted quietly. The priest took a deep breath, looked at Dina, who nodded. It was then that the priest, taking a deep breath, said, 'Kalidasa. And you must know him too. His is a name that will outlive us all.'

Atisa stared at the priest, unable to believe what he had just heard. So this was the famous dramatist, whose name had remained immortal through the centuries. Atisa wondered why he was on the run, but waited for Vasudeva to tell him more.

'Now that you know his identity,' said the priest, 'it is all the more important to save him. We thought it was the Sakas who were after him, but it's not them... we know it's not that. It is someone else who is so desperate that he will stop at nothing.' The priest spoke in low tones, always looking over his shoulder as if he would be overheard. 'Dina here, and then your mother too, mentioned a man on wings. And we know who it could be – someone from the court. Dipanna, a jealous rival, will do anything to harm him, and so it is important that Varahamihira the astronomer reaches Pataliputra and lets the king know everything. He will travel now that you have the valuable scrolls to give him. And maybe once you are in Pataliputra, you can find out things for yourself.'

There was no other sign of Kalidasa but his discarded quilt. Yet they knew the search couldn't ever be given up. It had to continue on his flying machine, though things were difficult in the night. There was not a moment to lose. Kalidasa had to be found and quickly too. So far, his sound catcher had only caught the movement of the wind, the clouds brushing against each other, the hooting of the elephant herds and the shrieking of the owls. He checked the sound catcher anxiously every now and then for any giveaway sound. The machine was full of the sounds of the night: the water below, the clouds scudding past, a few lone horsemen out at night, the elephants and the jackals, the hissing snakes and the rocks falling. There was nothing that would give away a man on the run or even a man chasing him. He had never seen a darker night. He dared not use his lantern for fear of being spotted as they now flew low over the forests, in search of Kalidasa.

The pathfinder shook his head grimly, 'There are just too many urgencies. The man Dipanna isn't here, and the poet is lost somewhere in the woods.'

He seemed suddenly lost in thought. 'But we must rush...

the boat isn't here, for Kalidasa is pretty much ineffectual at most things.' His lips twisted, but the amusement didn't linger long on his face. 'There's only one place where he could possibly be. Our people have guarded these mountains for a long time. Some of the Sakas gave us a bad name, and people believed we want to fight the king all the time but it's not true...'

Atisa was glad of Dina's presence in the machine, who directed Atisa to fly in a south-westerly direction, following the trail of the three stars. 'There is an old abandoned temple, away from the main road that leads westwards. In the past, Kalidasa spent some time there.' Dina explained that some parts of Kalidasa's long poem *Meghdoot* were written in the days he spent at that temple. It was the fastest he had flown anywhere, and Dina revealed that he had often escorted Kalidasa through the mountains to the west. This was how the princess and he met in secret.

The temple was quiet as they approached. Night had settled in thick, and dawn had not yet broken. Atisa yawned, and that caught on the sound catcher, and he also heard the sound of branches moving, the grass under his feet and the night insects all round. They took every step cautiously, not letting the temple out of sight. It was as they stepped on to the threshold, the bells tolling in the thin breeze, that they heard the scratching of quill on palm leaf. Kalidasa was bent over a palm leaf scroll, engrossed in his work, oblivious to everything, even to their arrival. And they stood at the door, just watching. Relief had made them fall silent. As Kalidasa leant forward to dip his quill into the ink, he sensed their presence and instantly a smile covered his face as he recognized Dina. 'You took a long while this time.' Dina rushed forward to embrace Kalidasa warmly, 'We cannot waste more time here. There is a man on your trail. We have to hide you away.' Kalidasa looked towards the palm leaf trembling on the floor, 'I have just finished the manuscript. The princess will be happy.' 'Yes, I understand,' said the pathfinder bowing, 'you must be happy too. She is already on her way to Pataliputra. But there is danger.'

He hesitated, not wanting to alarm Kalidasa, before he spread his hands wide in helplessness, 'A man is on your trail...'

'A man called Dipanna,' finished Atisa quietly. Kalidasa shrugged good-naturedly, 'He never gives up, does he?'

Atisa smiled weakly, his fatigue catching up with him suddenly. The temple floors were cool, and there were soft cotton carpets spread out that looked inviting. All around, there was the fragrance of jasmine and honeysuckle. He seemed to have flown a long while and wondered what his parents would say if he told them he had crossed the country several times. In the meantime, Kalidasa spread a blanket out and said they had to rest for the night. They were only too glad to take up his offer.

Kalidasa was safe, and while Dipanna could be anywhere near, for some hours they could afford to let down their guard. 'No one knows where this temple is. It almost vanishes into the mountains, and I am told it's visible only on clear moonless nights, when its spire actually glows green,' said Dina. 'Did Nurah fix up the lights for you?' asked Atisa, remembering the glow-worm-fixed kites that had proved such a help to him. But Kalidasa was writing again. Atisa heard his quill making a comforting scratching sound in the background as he felt his eyes close. It crossed his mind that it had been a while since he had seen Nurah.

Onward to Jhansi

Next morning, as the balloon unfolded and the machine swelled up, Kalidasa stared at it, in open-mouthed amazement. 'It is like something I have always imagined.' He smiled at them, oblivious to the danger that still lurked. Enthusiasm had brought on a shine to his eyes. 'You know the locals here believe that it was in this temple that Rama and Sita stopped on Ravana's flying machine as they were on their way back to Ayodhya.'

He looked from one to the other before he went on. 'I always thought I'd write about it. Do you know that the flying machine story is so ancient, even before our grandparents' time and even more.' 'Didn't you once tell me about it?' said the pathfinder. His tone was light, but he was looking worried. 'It's not safe, we have to get you out of here.' 'I am not sure but...'

This time Dina overrode Kalidasa's hesitation, 'You must not step out of the temple. You must not, not until I make sure.'

Then as he stepped out to check their surroundings, they were jolted by a loud elephant roar. This was followed at once by a pronounced trumpeting that seemed to come from everywhere and the sudden shaking of branches as birds scattered in alarm. 'They are here, the elephant herders,' said Dina in considerable relief. 'Some of the elephants can run fast, really fast, thunderous yet graceful. They will take you to

Pataliputra in no time.' 'On an elephant,' said Kalidasa, and he gulped. It was clear he was nervous about the prospect. Atisa was momentarily glad he hadn't been the only one.

Dina explained, 'The flying machine would be too risky. That man, who we know is on your trail, will stop at nothing. Then there are the Sakas, some of whom are fine archers and could try to bring the machine down. And in any case, the elephants will not be seen.' 'I will follow you anyway,' assured Atisa. Dina, however, still looked worried. 'You will have to take considerable risks; there is no cloud cover.' As they made their plans, the rustling around them increased. And out stepped Nurah from the dense underbrush, casually fixing his long top hat back on to his head. Dina gave him a mock salute, 'You do turn up at the oddest moments.' And Atisa grinned, 'We should have expected this.' 'He always goes,' said the pathfinder, 'where there is a good business opportunity... something I have never been able to understand.'

Nurah smiled absently. 'My young friend here,' he said pointing to Atisa, 'knows my methods. Did the kites work?'

'Too well,' Atisa replied. Nurah took his time, catching up on his breath as he sat under a tree, claiming that he had had a long journey after all. The pathfinder's impatience only grew at this and Kalidasa looked on, dazed. Atisa suspected that it was all deliberate on the poet's part. Kalidasa, he was sure, was writing in his head. 'I must go and look for the man who did all this...,' Dina said, fixing his quiver back on to his shoulders.

'Dipanna,' said Atisa, rising. 'Do you know what he looks like...,' asked Nurah, rummaging in his sack, 'apart from what the man in Ujjain told us? Anyway, here's a picture. I should have given it to you right away.' 'And how did you manage that?' asked Atisa. Nurah took him aside as he pulled out the black-and-white sketch from his sack, 'I found it, in the marketplace at Ujjain. I had to leave suddenly, and an artist there said I was to give it to you.' He handed it to Atisa, who waited to hear more, knowing Nurah relished telling stories and stretched these out as much as possible. He looked down at the scroll Nurah had held out and saw a thin face, a man with one eye smaller than the other. It was a sinister face, clearly someone to be wary of. Atisa was sure it matched the description given by the man they had met in Ujjain. Still he asked Nurah, 'But how did you know it was for me?'

'Hold it up against the light,' Nurah instructed. He held it up, so the sunlight fell on the palm leaf in a different way, and this time it altered the face in some way. The lips had lifted in a cruel smirk, and across his right cheek was a scar. Nurah nodded, looking pleased. 'At the marketplace in Ujjain, the artist said a woman had stopped there a long time ago and had asked him to draw the portrait from memory.' Atisa looked at the portrait, squinting as he did so, and Nurah spoke up again, 'You can tell who it is all right. And she had paid him quite generously too, with a fine Arabian horse, the best of its kind.'

He looked funnily guilty as Atisa looked up at him. Then he looked away as if to evade Atisa's gaze. 'There are many ways it could have come to me, or maybe I came upon it...,' Nurah finally said, and Atisa knew he was being deliberately enigmatic, 'and now let me get the elephants in order. You, my dear poet, can help yourself to the most docile and yet strongest of elephants here, the one I have promised to the princess.'

The poet blushed, and Nurah pressed on, 'She won't mind, I am sure.' The pathfinder stepped in then, 'Stop pulling everyone's legs,' and urging the poet forward towards the elephant who waited patiently, he said, 'You mustn't mind Nurah, and it will be all fine. The howdah will hold you fine, and this one is strong.' But Nurah was once again serious.

He looked far away as he said, 'Be careful heading towards Pataliputra. As long as the king knows nothing about Dipanna, we cannot rest easy.' He patted Atisa on the shoulder. Atisa would have to wait for the wind before he could fly away again. Nurah told him, 'You, young man, are not too far off course. You must head for Jhansi and meet the great, the great...'

And of course he had forgotten the astronomer's name again. Atisa, amused and impatient, gestured him to carry on, and Nurah looked apologetic. 'Make a case for me before the astronomer. So he forgives me, though getting his lost scrolls should make him happy.' Nurah made a convincing argument, but it somewhat added to Atisa's frustration. When would he go in search of his mother? But he had such a pleading look on his face, and the situation did look serious for Kalidasa, so he could not refuse. 'Take the route eastwards. You will know it from the flat plateau, the thin river Chambal, then the sound of the waterfalls and the wind in the deep forests. And then soon after, when there is a dip in the valley and where the river broadens, you will find the city of Jhansi. And the astronomer's house is easy to find at night, for he has invented a candle with a wick that burns very slowly and lasts through the night.' Nurah paused. It was as if the candle had made him wax poetic, 'A wick as thick as a rope, made of a special sap. You must travel just to see it. And imagine, at the end of it all, when you've handed him his long-lost scrolls and passed on information about Kalidasa, you'd forever have the king's gratitude.'

Twilight had already descended, but it carried a distinct menace. There were already heavy, dark storm clouds that hovered low and looked threatening. 'After the heat,' said Dina, 'comes the rain always. And this time it seems just more intense. But the weather will hold for a while. It's best you leave soon.'

They looked on in fascination as Atisa walked up the hill that hid the temple. Once he had a foothold to make the machine stand, he worked on his bellows, and the kites creaked as they opened, the machine widened and grew in size, the balloon first and then more slowly and ponderously the box cabin. As he stepped in, the kites stretched and spread like low wings. On the low dark clouds, once he was off, the kites worked like skates, and he bounced and skidded, constantly checking his lantern as it glowed purple in an increasingly grey sky. He had to ride low to reach Jhansi as quickly as possible, taking advantage of the storm clouds blown by the wind.

It was the sound of the river he picked up fast. The river spray rose high and struck him unexpectedly, and it was then that he knew that he was flying dangerously low. He pulled on his bellows, hoping to rise higher, but the wind was strong. He heard a scraping as his floor touched bare rock, the hard pebbles rose and made ringing noises against the balloon. The winds were sharp and hard, his machine swerved and bounced, and Atisa found himself being carried along a long distance down a low ravine. The wind in this narrow space was more vicious, screaming as it blew into the balloon folds, and it took him all his strength and hope to pull at the ropes. The balloon shuddered and heaved, the cabin thudded as it hit against the rocks every now and then, and below him, the lantern changed colour and lit up the valley in myriad ways.

He rode over a hill, over a rock shaped like a Roman soldier's helmet, and as he plunged low, he found the wind had gentled. The machine became stable and drifted more slowly now, and he saw the stars were out and that it was a clearer night than he had seen in days. He looked through his telescope and for a moment was startled, for someone with a telescope seemed to be looking out for him. At first it was to him a bizarre reflection, but it was clear that one telescope was clearly searching out another. Uneven-sized houses marked out the city of Jhansi as he neared, and he picked out the house where the glass face of a telescope had first blinked. It had a terrace that was the biggest of those around. A terrace, flat and uncluttered, quite unlike the other more fancy ones that came with domes and cupolas and even a fancy platform or two. All this terrace had along its balustrades were mirrors, which looked like pools of water in which the stars danced, caught in their own reflection.

Atisa was now more certain than before, that there was indeed someone with a telescope watching his every move. He floated down into the grounds, a vast empty space next to the boatyard. That telescope intrigued him, and he decided to wait in the grounds nearby, but it turned out to be a fairly longish wait. As he sat on the rocks, pulling his machine in slowly, he heard around him the sounds of a city about to sleep – the watchmen on their rounds, a few soldiers out on their horses and the bells of a temple ringing not too far away. And on the other side, where the forests began, he heard the howling of jackals, the trumpeting of elephants and when silence fell amid all this, the call of the few night owls.

Atisa still had the feeling he was being watched. Only moments later, he heard the sound of a horse, a steady clip-clop that his sound catcher picked up clearly. Someone coming surely and certainly, and he knew whoever it was, was looking for him. It had to be the person looking for him from the largest flat terrace in the city, the one who had a telescope as well. The rider tethered the horse and then spoke to it, and Atisa was startled to hear a girl's voice. 'He has to be here, somewhere very near. Let's see.' She was walking around, her voice rising and falling, and peering out from his hiding place, he saw she had lit a small candle and was doing calculations, tracing the numbers with a foot on the ground and without looking up said, 'It's all right, I know you are in there. I calculated it was so. Come on out.' She raised the candle and was looking in his direction. It was a girl in plaits, and she looked just about as tall as he was. She placed the candle on a rock, letting its wax settle, and waited, arms akimbo. He emerged, looking sheepish, but she didn't look threatening as she stood there. In fact, she was just as surprised to see him and smiled when he waved his hand tentatively at her. He tried out his Prakrit on her, 'I must show you that I am not armed.' She replied, 'You could not be. I saw you on the machine,' and she stopped, sounding excited and looking all around her. 'Can such a thing really fly?'

When he nodded, she said 'Yes,' and later told him, 'From the speed of your flying machine and where it probably landed, I did the calculations. Considering the circumference of your reach and the perimeter of distance that can be covered, I surmised that you would be around.' 'But you did not know how fast I could run or other things about me,' countered Atisa. 'That's right, I didn't. There is a lot of surmising. But within streams of probability, this is where I was likely to find you.'

'And what brings you here?' she asked suddenly. He was sure that if he told her that it was about his mother, she wouldn't be too surprised. In any case, she spoke too fast, and Atisa was glad he had remembered to put on his decoder. It was a bit difficult though. The decoder made her voice very mechanical, and the words buzzed and echoed in his ears, moments after she said them. It did seem she had too much to say. She stared as he dragged his machine from behind a rock and strapped it on his shoulder. 'Your mother, you were saying... of course it had to be her,' she said, and her words were breaking up as she moved from rock to rock, looking behind her often. 'But you will tell me by and by, about your mother. First come home. Father will be excited to see the machine, but oh...'

She stopped, and he saw she had become very serious. He knew it was Lilavati, the astronomer's daughter, and what she said next only confirmed it for him. 'My father is not in a very good mood. There is a trader who was supposed to come with some equipment for him... and some scrolls he was to deliver to a monastery but were unfortunately lost. The trader was supposed to get these, because my father is due to visit Pataliputra for the eclipse.' 'I have some of the stuff you need; the important scrolls your father lost.'

She stared at him, her eyes wide with amazement. 'You are indeed full of surprises. The scrolls that father lost?'

He nodded. 'It's quite a long story how I came by these scrolls. But Nurah had to rush off somewhere and it's best I...'

She laughed, interrupting him, and he knew then that he would always call her Lila. Somehow that made her nearer his time, but she wasn't to ever know that. 'Nurah, yes,' she was now saying, 'Father is quite upset with him. But I quite like the way you speak. And yes, father will be delighted. He was thinking he would need to rework them again to present to the king. Everyone, even in Pataliputra, is really afraid. But his research shows clearly that the eclipse has happened before, and nothing dangerous is to be associated with its occurrence.'

They walked through a winding path that led past a garden, and soon they were in front of a small mansion that looked abandoned, and she was leading him through, past a wicker gate. 'I left my horse here. He would have got very nervous if he had seen the machine.' She stood there and whistled, so loudly and clearly that Atisa was startled. It sounded like a train whistle caught on his sound catcher. 'There he is.' He turned to see a small brown pony come trotting up. 'We will take turns riding him, don't you worry,' she reassured. 'You must be tired after a long journey, and flying can take a lot of concentration.' He was surprised at how perceptive she was, but she was speaking up again. 'And since I am more familiar with this road going downhill past the rocks, I will hold Nitya. You just hold on to the saddle, for it can get very bouncy and jumpy.'

It did indeed make for a very awkward ride, Atisa holding on to the saddle and his machine trailing alongside. Somehow, the kites had opened up as the horse cantered down the hill path, and the glow-worm-like lights made the descent downhill far easier. 'You know the trader gave me these kites too. He is quite a resourceful guy but...,' and she went on to tell him of the candle with its magical wick that burnt all night long. 'He actually had the audacity to suggest that father set up a workshop to make more of these, for these would sell.' 'And father roared at him. "The temerity of the man," he said. "A great astronomer reduced to doing business..." It took quite an effort to calm him down,' said Lila, and they were still laughing as they reached the first houses on the outskirts of the town.

They passed darkened streets now, and in places the road narrowed as old houses leant down, and if they wanted, they could reach across and touch the columns on every house porch. They dismounted, for it was best to be quiet, and Lila held on to the horse Nitya, whose ears flapped and twitched as if he was following the conversation too. Then she said the most unexpected thing. 'Did you know when father and I were returning to Jhansi from Pataliputra, because he had gone to teach at the university there, we were joined by a magic woman?'

She bent and rubbed two stones together and produced a small fire. She held up the stones high, and the fire framed her narrow, serious face as she looked at him. It was strange to be looked at, Atisa thought, by a face he knew was 1800 years older than he was. 'You do look like her.'

She spoke slowly and clearly, and Atisa slowly taking off his decoder was glad to realize that he could indeed follow her.

'She said she wanted to pass on a message about someone she had found. But I think there was someone on her trail, perhaps she knew something. And then...,' she shrugged.

She turned to him, saw the worry on his face and shook her head. From the way she hesitated, he knew she wanted to say something more but wasn't sure. They turned a corner, moved into an even narrower lane, Nitya's steps behind them, a soothing trot. 'You are not to worry. The *daroga* got suspicious about your mother when she joined us, because of all the fears about the eclipse. But he is overzealous and making too much of all these rumours. He would turn up at almost every hour, saying he had to ask questions, see her documents. He even had secret guards posted here, till it became impossible for us to go out. And then we had to get her out secretly. The pathfinder called Dina came by...'

Atisa drew in his breath at the mention of Dina, but still he couldn't help but be worried about his mother. Lila said, reading his thoughts again, 'I shouldn't have told you all this. And the *daroga* is a bully. Remember never to be cowered down by him.' She patted his hand, urging Nitya on, and continued speaking in her high urgent voice, 'Don't worry, she's safe. Dina knows all the secret routes, the ways through the mountains, past the forests. He said he knew all the old...'

She dropped her voice, so it was almost a whisper, 'the old Saka routes, but the Sakas are the enemy. And we mustn't be overheard.' He managed a grin, somehow happy that his mother was safe. She winked, 'Or else it could get the *daroga* after us.' He smiled and because she had been so reassuring, he forgot to ask her about the other person, the man on wings who had followed his mother, the one who had made attempts on the injured man's life. Was he the same as Dipanna?

They were riding through the older denser parts of the city now, down streets that would lead to the main one that ran right through the heart of the city. As they took a sudden turn, past a darkened lane surrounded by immense quiet mansions on either side, they heard the sounds of a procession ahead. The houses with their immense shuttered gates and barred and curtained windows had muted the sounds. It had appeared like the sound from a distant temple, but once they stood at the corner, the sounds of cymbals, drums and chanting of hymns caught them unawares.

The horse came up to them, stopped abruptly and shied away, evidently scared by the sound. Lila pacified him as she explained. 'It's a new sculpture that has just been commissioned for the temple. It was to be installed, and I think the auspicious hour happens to be now.' The procession took its time, however, for it would stop every few minutes, as the music died away, and then in no time, the fanfare would begin all over again. At every street corner on the main road, policemen waited on horses, carrying batons. 'That's just part of the security,' she explained, as if she thought he was nervous. The policemen wore long, sweeping turbans, a short robe and tight pyjamas, and all of them wore long thick moustaches that only emphasized the menace on their faces. Their horses stomped, and sometimes the policemen twirled their moustaches and swung their batons from one hand to the other. They waited, barely hiding their impatience and Atisa was bemused. 'I didn't know you had traffic jams.'

Then he missed her reply because he was staring at his mother's face, on a poster fixed on the wall. He could read it clearly from where he was – the poster said that his mother was wanted for stealing a horse. Atisa gasped, knowing what this meant – the horse his mother had generously rewarded the portrait painter was in fact a stolen one. He recognized her clearly, though she was dressed like a magician, with a turban and a loose, flapping cloak, and her backpack made her look like a pirate of old. Lila saw it at the same time and stopped, so very suddenly that her horse stumbled, reared and tossed its mane. Then she had to lean forward to pat it.

There, there. Bother, bother. She chewed her lip. 'Father had expressly met the *daroga* after she left. He is a suspicious man and refuses to let up. Any stranger, especially someone who is practising magic, has to register. But she was evasive. She had to somehow reach the north-west, and the *daroga* kept snooping around. Now that she's gone, he's done this.' 'She looks nice though in that turban,' he said. His mother, he thought, was having quite an adventure of her own, though he did worry about her safety and where she was now. 'She had these things called boots on,' Lila chimed in. 'I was quite taken in by them. I did copy them and take them to the shoemaker, and he too was impressed.' 'Where is she?' asked Atisa, but he could not make himself heard above the din. 'The temple at Deogarh has invited sculptors from all over,' she bent to lean close and almost whispered in his ears. 'But father can tell you more about it. It is a secret construction, and the king is putting in a lot. The sculptors will be...'

But there was a blast of horns, and she turned away in annoyance, knowing she could not speak in all the din. Now the musicians were in a frenzy, and it was clear that they had had too much to drink. They weren't moving but swaying and dancing to their own beat, and if one of them stopped, others picked up, and in this way it went on. The soldiers watched them, stern and unmoving. It was obvious the road wouldn't be clear and empty for a long while yet. In the middle of all this, someone among the policemen, who looked just as fierce as the others, placed a horn on his lips, and its sound rose high and sonorous above the revelry, and its echo came bounding back to drown everything out again.

He brushed his moustache up again and said, 'All right, not too much. There may be noise, but not too much.'

Amid much laughter at that announcement, the dancing and swinging began all over again. 'Oh bother, that's him now, the *daroga*, the man I was telling you about,' Lila placed her hand over her mouth. 'We will be late, and father will be so upset, but we cannot let the *daroga* see us – he does have eagle eyes.'

But they found themselves trapped, for there were the rambunctious crowds ahead, and behind them were the tall, imposing walls of a mansion. 'We must hide... and quickly,' Lila whispered hurriedly, and as they ran back down the lane, the rolled-up umbrella made movement difficult. But Lila evidently thought on her feet. She patted her horse and whispered into its ears, 'Go home now, Nitya, go home safely.' She beckoned to Atisa, placed his flying machine rolled up into a tight umbrella against the wall and climbed up on it effortlessly, never losing her foothold once. The kites that stood out as square-shaped ledges held her securely. Atisa stunned at first followed suit and then pulled up the machine after him. She smiled, looking back, 'Nurah's kites, right? They are light and firm at the same time. They are much in demand here, and the *daroga* was thinking of banning them because they seemed to be in demand among thieves too. They could climb into buildings at will, using these. At least that's what the *daroga* claimed, and he even had a warrant out for Nurah, for supplying the evil equipment.' Atisa couldn't help but chuckle.

They were on a low terrace, fringed by flower pots and water barrels, and they could see the tight-knit procession below. They saw people making way as the *daroga* rode through, his sword held high over and above the crowd. The people appeared quite terrified of him, and some pressed against the walls as he passed. As Lila's horse, Nitya, made his way forward uncertainly as if lost, the *daroga* came to an abrupt halt. *Stop.* The sounds died away, the sound of hooves stilled and the air throbbed with menace. The last sounds of the cymbals died away, and even the clouds above stood unmoving and heavy. 'That's her horse, the pundit's daughter's.'

Beside him, Atisa heard Lila's angry mutter. 'He always calls father this, a pundit. He does more than a priest's job, and far busier really. He's a teacher, a guru.'

But Atisa urged her to lower her voice, for now the *daroga* was twirling his moustache, swishing with his sword, looking all around in a very threatening manner. 'The girl has to be somewhere around. Her horse is here.' He turned around his horse over and over again, and shouted out his command again, 'Clear the way and look for her.' He looked up, and for a moment, Atisa ducked back behind the wall, thinking he had been seen. They waited, knowing all the while it was getting late. His men darted away in futile search, and the procession was now utterly silent. The heavy smoke from the coir fire and incense sticks made things cloudy, and the drums and cymbals picked up, albeit slowly and hesitantly. The crowds took a long time to move down the street.

Finally, as some measure of quiet descended, it was the open terrace that gave Atisa the idea. He placed the machine against the wall, and once again stepped on the bellows, praying fervently it wouldn't make the screechy noise it sometimes did, which carried in quiet moments. The balloon swelled, moved over the water tanks, bobbed across the low walls, and the cabin stretched out, the ropes lengthened and Lila looked on with barely concealed excitement before she stepped in, in a hurry to fly away. In no time, they were up and off on the flying machine, letting it rise to its full height. 'Actually,' she said, watching Atisa pull apart the ropes to let the air sweep into the machine, 'the *daroga* does have a reason, though he is too arrogant a man to listen to other people's reasons. As we waited for Dina, I helped her figure out the direction to Peshawar, and we got her the best horse...' 'Stolen from the *daroga*'s stables,' finished Atisa as he picked up what she was saying. He couldn't believe his mother was a horse thief.

As they descended, Atisa saw the strangest thing. It was a shadow moving along the walls, gingerly and cautiously, almost like a giant spider, and as the balloon touched the terrace floor, he saw the shadow slipping away, in a smooth, gliding manner. The shadow jumped from roof to roof and as he looked on, was gone in a jiffy. Lila looked puzzled too. 'There was something, wasn't there?'

He nodded. Someone had indeed seen them and then had been alarmed by the sight of the balloon descending. Then, whoever it had been, had made as quick a getaway as possible. But all was quiet now, and Atisa didn't want to alarm her. Once the balloon came to a complete halt, he heard on his sound catcher the sound of pattering footsteps, followed by a low whistle, and after that, again the long silence that he was so getting used to. And as they went inside, past the terrace he had first noticed from his telescope, down a circular staircase, Lila said, 'Maybe it was just a cat.' Then she was running down the stairs, her voice picking up, her excitement palpable, 'Father, we are back.'

The Astronomer
Varahamihira

'There's father. He is still working,' she said, over her shoulder, 'though actually he is waiting up for me.' They saw him as they ran down to the first floor, into a central courtyard around which were the rooms arranged in perfect order. The astronomer called Varahamihira was hunched over some scripts, peering close as he read. His shadow had darkened one entire corner of the wall. He had looked up as he heard the whooshing and whistling sound of the machine landing on the terrace just overhead, and now he rearranged his scrolls and looked at them, his eyes twinkling. He seemed unfazed by the presence of a stranger or the fact that they arrived by balloon. He pointed to a lit-up mirror, and Atisa saw it looked right up through a chimney on to the terrace. As he rose to his feet, Atisa saw he was tall and that he often ran his fingers through his long grey beard as he spoke.

'I could see you through that.' He smiled thinly and his eyes still twinkled as he explained, 'So I had ample time to hide my surprise.' Atisa gasped. He had no idea Varahamihira could possibly have seen it. 'Your balloon really is a most unique thing. It is lighter and doesn't have the weight to pull it back to earth.'

'Father, he...'

'Daughter, did that...?'

And they stopped. Atisa realized they were talking about the same man, the *daroga,* and at the same time, before they began all over again. 'He hasn't...' 'Not again.'

They stopped, and Lila held up her hand. 'Father, it's all right. We didn't mean to be late.' 'The idiot,' finished Varahamihira, but Lila was quick to placate him. 'Father it's all right. He did try and hold us up, but we managed to get away... we had the machine after all.' 'Ah yes, and I am very pleased to make your acquaintance.' Varahamihira looked at Atisa, and suddenly an idea brought a gleam into his eyes. 'I was wondering if I could take it with me to watch the eclipse closely.'

Lila and Atisa exchanged a look of startled surprise. 'Father, you can't mean it. I mean it's difficult to fly. I saw him do it. It's hard to manage against the wind.' 'Yes, I know,' he smiled wistfully, fingering his long beard. 'It would take me a long time to pick up skills like that, but it is a most fascinating machine. I need to leave immediately though. The king has specifically requested for me, especially as the eclipse is near.' He looked preoccupied as he rushed on with his words, 'People are worried, and they think I can reassure them.' That made Atisa remember the lost scrolls, and Lila did too, clapping her hands for his attention. 'Father, oh I had to tell you...'

But a strange, secretive look came over her face. 'There is something I am working on as well, and Atisa here is to help me with that.' 'Ah yes, the telescope especially.' Varahamihira smiled at his daughter, 'You have your heart set on perfecting that.' Only Atisa saw that his smile was sad and serious at the same time. 'That is why he is here, isn't he? You might have told me before. It is a good thing then for us, and we are very glad you are here.'

Barely had he finished when they heard an imperious knocking on the door and he frowned, his bushy eyebrows settling together, making him look like someone to be wary of. There was the stamping of a horse's feet and some whispering. Someone spoke in a loud and haughty voice, 'Oh great master, cherished gem of the king Vikramaditya, for the reasons of security, please open up.' A trembling servant rushed out from behind a column, 'It's that evil *daroga*. Always troubling us. It just does not matter to him that it is quite so late at night now.' He turned to Lila, 'Elder sister, they always pick on us when we are out in the market as well. He thinks we are harbouring the Sakas. Ever since that lady came, he thinks we are hiding something and up to no good.' The frown on Varahamihira's face became even darker. Atisa realized why Nurah was so afraid of displeasing him. 'He should do things that really matter, that *daroga*.' He had raised his voice, and the knocking on the door was louder than before. 'Have him shown inside.'

The servant hesitated, 'But Guru, it's late...' He ended lamely, looking from father to daughter, and it was Varahamihira who grumbled a reply, 'It's all right, have him shown in.' Barely had the heavy bolts on the main door been lifted when the *daroga* barged in, his feet hard on the stone floor, and he stopped when he caught sight of Atisa and Lila. He rubbed his hands in glee and settled his turban more securely on his head, 'Aha and here we have you, the traitors in our midst.' 'How dare you call anyone a traitor?' and Varahamihira rose, and his thunderous voice rolled out, making even the *daroga* stop in surprise. 'If there is any traitor, it is you. He is here to make observations on the eclipse, a mathematician from the land of...'

He broke out in a bout of coughing, and Lila hastened towards her father. 'You have agitated him considerably,' she turned furious eyes on the *daroga*. 'The king will be upset to hear this.' For the first time, Atisa saw fear in the *daroga*'s eyes. Varahamihira raised his voice again, 'The eclipse will be the most wonderful thing ever. Nothing like it has ever been recorded in our texts. And you dare interfere in such business. And he is our revered guest from the land of...'

Again he broke out into coughs, and the *daroga*'s eyes were now wide in wonder as he looked at Atisa. 'Isn't he a little young?'

'Age has nothing to do with the mind, oh poor *daroga*,' countered the astronomer, 'Your sword, your position and your false swagger may cause fear, but they impress few. It is the mind that decides everything.' The *daroga* swallowed his pride and also the retort he had ready, acknowledging defeat for now. He left but not before he delivered a half-veiled warning to Lila. 'You don't try and get smart. I will still get hold of that horse thief.' As Atisa made to protest, she clamped a hand on his wrist, silencing him as she looked up roundly at the *daroga*, 'Considering how wrong you have been in most of your speculation, don't you think you are getting yourself into trouble? She has left on an important mission to give vital information to the king about the Sakas. If you are so suspicious, you could do that as well.' He gave his moustache a last twirl before he left. Only when he had finally left, and as the sound of his entourage died away, did Lila turn and tell her father about Atisa's reasons for being there, while Atisa thanked him for saving him in front of the *daroga*. Father and daughter exchanged glances full of mischief, and before the astronomer returned to his work, pointing ruefully at his scattered scrolls, he patted Atisa in a friendly manner and told him not to worry. 'Your mother actually went towards the north-west. You see, there's Fa-hsien who's due to visit India. And we felt this was the best time for her to escape. Once Fa-hsien comes here, and because of the eclipse, the borders would be specially patrolled and sealed.' Atisa felt sure that both were hiding something from him. It was only as

Lila helped the house servants prepare his room and arrange for the water pitchers to be filled up that she revealed more. The fragrance from the incense sticks wafted around them as she spoke. 'She was running from something or someone. A person who had tried to kill someone had also seen her and, in fact, traced her here to Jhansi. He had warned her already. She had to get away. We urged her then to move to the north-west.' Atisa longed to be asleep, but it was a new place and his sound catcher picked up the oddest noises. For Atisa it had already been a long journey since his escape from the ship, and there were worries crowding his mind. No sooner had he drifted off to sleep than he was startled awake by a thunderous sound, a boom that first had his sound catcher vibrating and a second later, he heard the splintering sound of glass breaking. It was as if a chandelier had plunged several feet or a glass planet had exploded into shards. This was followed by the eerie sound of someone crying, and on the sound catcher, its effects were amplified to sound like the repeated rush of waves on rocky shores. Before Atisa hurriedly lowered the volume of the sound catcher, he heard Varahamihira's voice, booming like a foghorn. 'How dare you sneak in?'

'I was...'

The man who replied was obviously very frightened and blubbered in his nervousness. 'No, I was just curious.'

'Tell us the truth, you rogue.' The servants were now awake and threatening him, taking turns to hurl accusations at him. 'I was curious about the machine, I saw it high in the sky.'

'You rogue, you liar.' This time it was the cook who made to hit him again. 'You are the one who has been pilfering stuff from the kitchen.'

The man shook his head again nervously, and there was a terrified banging of the doors. 'Great master, we heard there had been a break-in.'

The thief looked even more terrified and tried to hide behind a column. 'Please don't tell the police. They will skin me alive, great master.' 'Why are you here then?' Atisa asked in the most threatening manner he could assume.

'I was told by the *daroga* of the presence of strangers,' he evaded his eyes, 'and was told to check.' 'We are sparing your life and not handing you over this time because it's not really your fault,' said Varahamihira, who was trying hard not to grin. The *daroga* seemed an indefatigable sort, who refused to give up on his suspicions. It was already morning, and as they had dried bread and jaggery in warm milk for breakfast, and the sun made a lean shadow on the sundial in the garden, Atisa picked out some familiar noises on the sound catcher. 'Nurah has to be near,' said Atisa, 'I can hear him blowing on his trumpet.' It made Varahamihira snort in irritation. 'About time too, he makes amends for all his goof-ups.'

Nurah appeared in his usual manner, his top hat rising over the boundary wall. He was at the head of a fairly large troop of horses and a herd of goats, but he looked so very upset that Atisa couldn't quite ask him about the elephants he had last seen him with. Nurah doffed his hat, looked into it in the deepest misery and then broke the news. 'I have to say that Ghatakapura the architect, and one of the gems of King Vikramaditya's court, has been killed mysteriously. He was travelling to Deogarh to work on the temple but was found dead on the way. His horse returned without him. There are no suspects, but everywhere there are guards. So all this held up my progress, taking me a day more than usual. There is just too much fear and suspicion. And we know who to suspect, but there is no proof yet.' He exchanged glances with Atisa, while Varahamihira maintained a sombre silence. 'We need the great astronomer to move to Pataliputra immediately.' His words fell into a thick silence, but Nurah waited for no response as he held out a scroll for Atisa. 'And you might want to go to Pataliputra as well,' and he nodded meaningfully at Atisa, 'to warn the king that this is the man we are looking for.' And with that he produced yet another copy of the portrait of Dipanna.

'I need to hurry,' he said. 'Ask no questions dear boy and you will be told no lies.' For Atisa was puzzled as to how he had got yet another copy of the portrait. The pencil lines wouldn't come on in his fingers, and yet this seemed to be an exact copy. But Nurah wouldn't let on and wouldn't even look Atisa's way, as if he was afraid of giving something away. 'We all need to hurry. The borders with the north-west have already been closed, as you well know. There is no way you can cross over to meet your mother.' He saw Atisa's stricken face and gently smiled. 'All I can assure you, just as the great astronomer did too...,' he coughed as he had forgotten the name again, 'is that your mother is indeed safe.' When he saw Atisa wasn't really convinced, he dismounted and then looked deep into his long hat, the way he often did, before he went on, 'News spreads, my dear boy, faster than you imagine. You may come from a different time, I mean place...'

He broke off, while Lila looked puzzled and excited. 'From a different time?'

This time Nurah changed the subject more decisively than before, 'I need to move on. I have to show the great monk Fa-hsien a different route from the border. The Saka tribes in the north-west might be inclined to trouble him. And he may have news for you, dear boy. Just the news you are looking for.'

This time he exchanged a significant wink with Atisa. 'And now I must meet the *daroga,* to intimate him about my presence – he believes in being so officious – and then move on to the north-west. And mind that portrait, you might find it useful in Pataliputra.'

Later in the night, looking up at the sky, the astronomer showed the first signs of being worried. He pointed to the sky and murmured almost to himself, 'There will be unexpected rainfall. I hope it doesn't hold up my departure.'

The Strange Boat Journey

Nurah's plans were to leave early the next morning with his troop of magnificent horses. Atisa couldn't help asking Lila, his curiosity getting the better of him, 'What did he do with the goats that were also with him?'

'The herders will take care of them,' said Lila, 'It's a kind of arrangement.' When he looked puzzled, she shrugged, 'All right, as you may have guessed he does important work for the king and the government. His flocks and his trading activities give him adequate cover to gather information and pass it on to the right people.' But all plans to depart were delayed as the rain began to fall steadily in moments. The drizzle turned into a steady curtain of rain, with an unrelenting whooshing noise. Varahamihira's plan of setting out for Pataliputra in the horse-drawn carriage specially arranged for him was delayed, and Nurah too looked increasingly anxious when he returned from the *daroga*'s office, for the rain refused to ease. It was in the midst of all this that the *daroga* turned up soon after, with his usual fanfare, followed by his trident-bearing horsemen. One of his men unfurled a scroll, and at a signal from the *daroga,* he read it aloud. *You must submit information on whoever is leaving with you. These are the orders of the king and all those who obey his orders dutifully.* With that the man folded up his scroll, and the *daroga* looked self-importantly around, twirling the club he wielded. He sneered as his eyes lingered on Nurah's entourage, 'You do seem to have a whole lot of people with you.' Varahamihira sighed, though he had no intention of creating a scene. The *daroga* was a nuisance and could delay his departure on one flimsy pretext or another. He saw Atisa's discomfort and Lila's impatience and replied in an even, calm tone, 'You are only holding me up, oh loyal servant of the great Vikramaditya. And it seems the rains will only get heavier. The king will not be very pleased to hear that you were responsible.'

The *daroga* turned sullen, and his raised hand dropped to his side. He spoke in more even tones, 'I was only advising caution. I have secret information. There is danger.' He turned his horse around, and at a signal, his men fell in line once more. A few steps later, he turned his horse around once more in a complete circle, to deliver a last veiled threat, with a quick look at Atisa, 'I will keep an eye on you, young man. There is no way you can pull a fast one on me.' Atisa was taken aback, and Lila looked thoughtful. 'Father, there is something sinister afoot. And the *daroga* is right in his own way. Someone in the king's court, the architect Ghatakapura, is now dead, believed to be murdered. And we must take every precaution.'

Her voice died away, and she looked very despondent, and Atisa realized she too couldn't bring herself to talk of Kalidasa. He longed to tell her about Dina and how the pathfinder knew all the secret routes, but he refrained when he caught Nurah's gaze on him. The trader shook his head ever so gently, as if warning him that there was a time for everything.

Varahamihira, glancing up at the skies, hardly noticed all this. In fact, he looked most woebegone, and that was when Atisa came up with a plan. Sizing up the urgency of the situation, and hoping his audacity would not upset the great astronomer, he said, 'It can still be done. We just use a different route.'

Varahamihira turned and stared at him, but Atisa did not cower under that unblinking look. 'A different route? Do you know we have to reach on time?' Lila shook her head, hiding her amusement, 'You are not suggesting that we go by balloon, are you?' Atisa also shook his head. It was impossible to conceive the three of them travelling in his flying machine. It was a sturdy machine but it had limits, and yet most of the roads had been declared unsafe and were being heavily patrolled as well. Progress would be slow by any measure. Atisa nodded, putting on a determined look. He hoped it made him look older and more convincing. 'It can be managed – a boat propelled by horses and my machine flying overhead. I am sure the rain will let up once we've crossed some distance,' he said. 'And we'd save time too. Let's try and work it out like this.'

It was Varahamihira's turn to look amused, as he considered the younger man's idea. 'Looks like you have an exciting new invention in mind.' Atisa nodded pleased, breathless with excitement. He was sure it would work. The horses, some of them borrowed from Nurah, were arranged in line. A servant even got the *daroga*'s assistants to get the thana's horses into action too. At some plainly uttered commands, the horses, sturdy creatures that they were, jumped into the water, the boat ropes attached to their saddles. They would ride with shallow currents, and the boat with Varahamihira in it would be safe. While overhead, the machine tied to the boat would follow the same journey. 'You remember this, there is danger,' shouted one of the *daroga*'s men from the bank.

The winds were high, and the lift-off made Lila laugh in exhilaration. Atisa kept a careful lookout through his telescope, while she stood at the other end of the cabin, looking through her own.

Atisa thought he saw forests move, as they flew away, the boat rocking along, in a gentle, bobbing fashion below. To him the trees appeared to move in one continuous wave, and the sound catcher picked up the different sounds of the wind as it moved through the trees and the roar of the waters below, striking against the rocks and lapping against the boat. The roads stretched out beyond the hard brown hills, and the river flowed neat and blue, cutting its way through the rocks. The astronomer sat under the canopy, unperturbed, almost oblivious. He was looking over his scrolls, and every time the spray rose high over the boat, he flicked it away with a bare touch of a finger. It was a while later that the sound catcher picked up the sound of the horsemen on the road, and soon there were more. Somewhere to the east, an outpost was clearly visible, and the horsemen changed places, and two more rode out in their place. They rode together part of the way and then separated, and it seemed one was coming straight down the road, headed for the north-west. 'They are from Pataliputra, there is no doubt,' said Lila who hadn't for a moment taken her eyes away from the telescope. There was something of a steely determination in the way they moved. Atisa thought about Dina again and wondered if he and Kalidasa were safe in the forests. Below, they heard the horses still at work, splashing through the waters. A few rocks fell as they moved ahead, and the noise resounded on his sound catcher like an avalanche. 'This can get to be a choppy journey, I surmise,' said Varahamihira, barely giving them an occasional glance. 'Don't be worried.' Varahamihira's deep gravelly voice echoed against the rocks by the riverbank and was magnified by the catcher so it sounded as ominous as thunder. At times, Atisa had to fly low to guide the boat. They were now in hill country, and here the river Betwa flowed swiftly, with unpredictable currents, and from above, the rocks that lay deceptively beneath the water could be clearly seen. They needed to sail with care all the way to Orrchha, where they would stop for a while at the old stone palace right by the river Betwa. The river quieted down as they moved through the plateau and as evening fell.

The horses neighed, splashing playfully now in the waters. From afar, they saw the deserted palace of the old kings, its grey stone mellow in the soft light. Atisa looked up at the stars and wondered how easy it was for him to always slip through time. The balloon bobbed in the wind; he had let it swell up to its fullest, and the wind played in its many folds, first in quick rushes and then more slowly, in a growing stillness. It was this that warned him, the quiet that came far too quickly. This was followed a moment later by the shrill neighing of the horses, as the waters gentle some moments before, rose all around like small fountains. He felt the spray rise and catch him on the face. There followed the sound of skittering stones, which appeared like loud knocking on the sound catcher. The neighing picked up, the sound of galloping horses mingled with the falling rocks and it all ended with a strange, sinister rumbling that came from within the bowels of the earth. The sound catcher magnified all this to terrifying levels.

In all this, the boat seemed to be the only place that looked safe, and though it bounced and jumped, it did not turn over. Varahamihira held on to his scrolls and looked on, his expression giving nothing away. Lila was calming the horses, calling out to them in her clear, high voice. They couldn't hear her, but soon the neighing died away, though the horses still looked skittish, their tails flicking nervously, as they tossed their manes and moved close to each other. Atisa and Lila moved closer to the boat, directing the machine carefully. The ropes drawn taut and tied to the boat's hull and its front, and the boat's cabin halfway, made for a strange sight. Atisa's flying machine shook in the wind and bounced and heaved, but otherwise did not behave too erratically. The astronomer motioned them all to stay calm. 'We are away from the stones and safe,' he said. But beyond the boat, Atisa and Lila could see the river caught in chaotic eddies and circles. The rocks

tumbled down from a height and descended with a splash. The earth seemed to move in a violent seesawing motion; it shifted to one side and then moved back again. Atisa saw the balloon over his machine veer erratically. He pulled at the strings and was immensely relieved, for the strings remained securely attached to the boat. And then just as suddenly as it had begun, the earthquake died away. At the end, it struck a weird musical note. The skittering died away, the waters settled down somewhat and they realized that the sound was fainter because they had also drifted a considerable distance. Only the birds circled overhead, and of Nurah or his horses, farther away on the road, there was now no sign. The fast-flowing river and wind currents pushed the machine and the boat along. It was almost like being in a speedboat. The waves surged high at times, the foam rose like thick blobs of silver and the river flowed swiftly, forming whirlpools and eddies, dipping in places, barging against hidden rocks and swirling against the boat time and again. But its force had gentled, and the river wasn't as fiery as it had been moments ago. 'Most unusual,' said Varahamihira, shaking the water off his scrolls again. 'It has yet to be ascertained whether such natural phenomena have any link with the eclipse, and in particular with the baneful movement of the planets.' 'Mars is whimsical, does things its own way. This time of year, every other year, Mars has usually been a bit brighter than it is now. In the records left by my forefathers, my mother and before her, her grandmother, made these observations. They noted that during the reign of the great king Ashoka, some two centuries ago, Mars was brighter than before. It seemed to eat up all the rain clouds, it competed with the moon in the night sky and even our winters, the kind of winters we know in the plains, were mild. But the relief, because the winters were no longer as harsh, did not last. It gave people too much to think about.

The nights were always more boisterous than before, with the circus and the night artists who were always performing. Then there were the aimless soldiers in the bars and pubs, engaging in duels and fights with one another, and so it wasn't really a peaceful time, though the weather was quite so.'

Atisa and Lila listened, fascinated by this story. Varahamihira guffawed, seeing the rapt expression on their faces, 'It is just a story of course. It would be so easy to predict events in future if one could relate a planet's presence in the sky to our own lives. But since then, Mars has shown changes, or else its brightness has diminished. And I wasn't sure why.' At this point, his eyes lit up, 'Then I realized from a reading of the old texts and records that there had to be other objects in Mar's path. Even Lila's telescope,' he smiled at his daughter, 'told me something. There had to be other objects in its path, another planet or perhaps the moon in the way, and then I realized it would be the most unusual eclipse of all. Something I had to write about, even record, in the interests of posterity, for such an event is rare and happens only once in several lifetimes.'

They did not realize, by the time he had finished speaking, that they were in calmer waters. The cabin stood still, and in the distance, they saw the red walls of the fort, simmering in the morning light. It seemed the earthquake had never happened. It had been the most unusual ride Atisa had ever had. Atisa and Lila pulled down the ropes, the wind buffeting them gently from all sides, and the sound of it on the sound catcher was like the rumblings inside a cave. The river was wider now. And on the banks were the ghats and the small boatyards where the fishing boats now rested. The river Betwa met the Yamuna at this point, just beyond where the fort walls ended, and flocks of storks flew down and all around, curious about the balloon. The wind caught in the dark and dense rosewood trees and made an eerie whistling noise. The trees bent in unison, and that was when they could see right through past the plateau and the empty dry plains that led to the mountains to the east and north. 'It's very slippery,' said Atisa, reassuring Lila, as they tried to come to grips with the rough balloon ropes, frayed now because of the repeated buffeting by the strong winds they had encountered. Once in Pataliputra, he knew he would have to mend these again. She was talking with her telescope fixed to her eye. 'Nurah's herd far away is quite massive now,' she said. 'I think the tribesmen are all headed for the west.' 'Yes, the Sakas don't dare attack them,' said the astronomer, 'The herdsmen are lifesavers in every way.' 'Look,' said Lila suddenly, and she pointed with her telescope, asking Atisa to do the same, 'Do you see what I am seeing?'He adjusted Daedalus' telescope and put it to his eye. In a direction opposite to where the herds were, he saw a procession, an orderly line, and among them men carrying palanquins too. He zoomed in for a closer look, thanking silently his father Gesar for his many innovations on a very old telescope. He could see they were white-robed monks, all of them carrying bamboo umbrellas. Some of them walked in pairs, balancing rods on their shoulders, and these held scrolls, heavily rolled up like sacks. 'It's Fa-hsien, father.'

Varahamihira looked up sharply, and a pleased expression appeared on his harsh, craggy face. 'I hope he will be in time for the conference. It would be most exciting to have him there and to discuss what the scientists of his country think about this.' 'He's coming with a fairly large entourage, father.'

Varahamihira laughed, 'Maybe he wants to take away as many texts from here as possible. But it would be a good exchange of knowledge.' Atisa stared at the panorama unfolding before his telescope in fascination. There were the rocky hills, the uneven plateau, with its rounded knolls, the stray copses of trees that appeared every once in a while, simmering pools that looked like sunken mirrors, villages with their colourfully painted walls and temple towers with orange flags on top. He glanced over low stupas, some as old as five hundred years and more. He spotted deer herds on the move. When he turned his camera westwards, there was no sign of Nurah. Low hills had appeared on the west, and they stretched for long miles. He hoped Nurah would have some news of his mother.

'The monks will travel till Kannauj and take the boat down the Ganga to Pataliputra,' said Lila. They could no longer see the monks after a while. Houses and small temples appeared like low blocks every once in a while, and there were the horsemen on the dusty roads, clearly in a state of alert. His reverie was interrupted by a low long piercing whistle. Someone shouted, 'Hey there, you do be careful. We don't want to have a mid-air collision.' Atisa had to turn in surprise, for he heard something within earshot and unexpectedly very close. He saw a boat, and it was also pulled by strings just like theirs, and flying overhead was an immense flock of cranes pulling it along. The man who had shouted out reclined in his boat, wrapped in a long cloak, and there were attendants clustered around him, holding his scrolls, his quills and even a spittoon. He put down his long whistle once he had their attention.

Then he cupped his hands around his mouth and hollered out, 'I don't know how comfortable you are, but in this boat, I have every comfort one can dream of.' Varahamihira only smiled absently, 'Perhaps you got the idea from us.' 'Never mind him,' said Lila smiling at Atisa's stupefaction. 'That's Vaaruchi, the astronomer. There is always some ribbing between father and him.'

'These are prized Siberian cranes,' Vaaruchi said, agitated by their indifference, and he stood up so very quickly in his indignation that the boat almost capsized. The cranes flew up and cackled in sudden disarray, and Atisa noted how the ropes had actually been chained to their feet. He thought this rather cruel and then raced to get his machine out of the way as spouts of water shot up.

There was alarmed shouting all around, and the sound catcher made it all appear as if they were in a crowded football stadium. The cranes screeched and called to each other, and the sounds mingled with the wind caught in the balloon and other shouts. Atisa looked down and realized that a flotilla of boats had sailed out on the river. With armour-clad soldiers having spears and feathered arrows in their quivers, and the boatmen in their colourful attire, the river looked suddenly very alive. 'We are here on the king Vikramaditya's orders. It is our duty to specially escort you to Pataliputra,' shouted across a soldier, and as Atisa looked on, he saw the boats were draped with the regalia of the Gupta dynasty. 'The reasons for this security are more serious than I thought,' muttered Varahamihira to himself, and his words were picked up by the sound catcher; 'evidently the threat to lives is a very serious concern.'

'Yes, father it has to be. And then the great Fa-hsien is expected to visit the country, and nothing should appear in a bad light.' 'True, I agree with you. But nothing should be excessive, even caution. Fear can stifle the mind and action like nothing else.' The soldiers on the boats around them were indeed watchful. They stood on the deck, armed with their bows and arrows, keeping a watchful eye. They checked every boat that passed and refused to let on the reasons for their search. Atisa couldn't but think of the modern-day security systems that were now such an integral part of every travel. The boats sailed in the middle, flanked by the soldiers' boats. They passed villages and everyone came out to watch, but they kept their distance. The forests that appeared on either side were still too.

Along the ghats, they also saw yogis in different postures of penance. One stood on his head, glaring up at the flying machine and waved threateningly at it. They also sailed by a huge fire that had been lit. Smoky black clouds filled the sky; this turned to a dense black fog that soon made everyone cough. Near them, there were also sadhus standing in a line, sprinkling holy water and chanting in unison.

'Pray, great sages, your fire is causing immense distress,' said the soldiers. The sadhus glared at the soldiers instead. 'We are praying for good things. Don't you know about the eclipse?'

'It might not bring in bad things,' said Varahamihira loudly. Vaaruchi had fallen asleep once again. Fanned by his attendants, he lay in comfort, snoring heavily. 'There is really no connection,' the astronomer repeated. Atisa looked down at the two sides caught in a fascinating debate across the river. But the closer they came to Pataliputra, the reasons for the ominous atmosphere soon became clear. One of the Nine Gems had been mysteriously killed, and even now, there was no clear news of where Kalidasa could be, though his disappearance was obviously a strictly guarded secret.

In the King's Court

Pataliputra came into view from a long way off. The city was lit up with candles and low fires that were visible from miles away. It was an island in the ocean of darkness, as if the stars themselves had dropped down and pinned themselves to the earth. For the next few days, the city would remain lit up at night on the king's orders. Everyone waited in equal dread and anticipation of the eclipse, when the earth would plunge into total darkness. As they drew nearer the city, they saw that everywhere the people were out in the streets. They saw lanterns strung up everywhere, and flares rose high at every street corner. There were all kinds of acrobats, jugglers, trapeze artists, fortune tellers and magicians performing. It was a bizarre scene of unending festivity. Fire performers swallowed up blazing torches without turning an eye, there were jugglers playing with fire balls and the sky was ablaze with colours of every kind. Inside the king's palace, there were dancers, whose bejewelled dresses reminded Atisa of the stars again, as he looked down from the courtyard while pulling the machine in.

Then Lila pointed out to him as she led him into the king's assembly, 'In such assemblies, the Nine Gems are always present... jewels of the kingdom in every way, except that...'

Her voice trailed away and she said quietly, 'there are two who are not here.' In spite of the revelry around, Atisa could sense the seriousness in the watching assembly. He read it in the faces of the men and women who were being cajoled to join in the dancing, and only some did, though in a forced manner. And then with a flurry of trumpets, and the beating of heavy drums, the king arrived. Atisa drew in his breath. He was about to see a king he had read much about. King Vikramaditya had battled away enemies, saved his kingdom and had challenged even vampires and ghouls who had dared deceive him time and again. The king was indeed magnificent, dressed in a carefully draped silk dhoti that shone like a mirror itself, and there was an intricately embroidered shawl that he gracefully draped over his shoulder. The assembly rose to honour him, the dancers stopped and in one move, they bowed before him. The sound of bangles clinking as one, and then the sound of drums picking up and conch shells blowing, had an instant effect. All fear seemed to have dissipated at the king's arrival. The king waited for the applause to die down, and then he spoke. 'Tonight we are all here. Tomorrow and the days that follow are vitally important. We must be careful and prepared till the day of the eclipse.' He stopped and corrected himself, 'night rather.' There was a rumble of low laughter. 'What it could mean for us and how we respond,' the king went on, his eyes moving from one face to another, 'will be assessed, generations later. But there is nothing to fear, no cause for alarm in all the unexpected events we have been faced with. As our great scientists have said, there is really nothing in the coincidence.' There was a murmur, evidently a voice of protest; the king raised his eyebrows. He read the discontent on some faces and went on, 'Evidently, some of the great astrologers disagree, and this should be a most interesting debate.' He smiled as he leant back on his cushions on the throne. And then he said, 'Though there are some things the astrologers haven't been able to explain too well.'

He waited for perfect silence to fall, before he asked the waiting assembly, 'Such as... where is Kalidasa?

And the great monk Fa-hsien should have been here. But I am told he has been forced to delay his journey, perhaps by our enemies.'

At once, the whisper swirled around the courtroom. The dreaded name had been taken. It could only be the Sakas who would so want to spite the king. They were the enemies who had sworn the king's destruction ever since Vikramaditya, then a prince, had disguised himself as a woman and entered the Saka camp. He left having killed their king in revenge. The Saka king had dared ask for the Gupta queen as hostage, and only the prince had dared oppose that. And while the Sakas had been defeated in every battle since then, and no longer dared march against the king Vikramaditya, they remained constant irritants. Atisa remembered all that he had encountered thus far: Nurah's warnings, Dina's watchfulness, the bandits who had kidnapped them, the archer on the ship and then the suspicion of the overzealous *daroga*. The guards at the palace tower had been cautious as well, as they had approached. They had demanded a special inspection of the flying machine, and only Varahamihira and Lila's presence had assured them an easy passage. 'Let the debate begin.' With a final clash of the cymbals, an absolute silence fell. But as the audience took its seat, amid murmurings and low laughter, there was a buzz towards the entrance. A courtier rushed forward, and as the curtains draping the facade were lifted, an attendant made a sensational announcement.

'Your majesty, the best of kings, the great monk is here.' It made the three of them start up in surprise. Fa-hsien walked with hesitant steps down the aisle. He wore a long cloak, and he made his way forward, holding on to a stick, urged on by his assistants. He wasn't old in the least, but he was indeed very tired and looked drained of all energy. He took every step with infinite slowness, walking between half a dozen or so retainers, who hovered around him, chanting verses and sprinkling holy water. 'He did get here kind of fast, but he looks very tired,' whispered Lila. 'Yes, there is something to this,' said Varahamihira. 'I did see him through the telescope,' said Lila, 'and things looked okay…'

Atisa completed her unfinished sentence, 'I do hope he is all right.' Varahamihira raised his hand, and they realized that they had been talking a bit too loudly. 'The king must have Dhanvantri, the royal physician, examine him.' But everything was interrupted by the fanfare of trumpets that rang out loudly, formally welcoming the monk into their midst. 'On behalf of the great king and the empire of Magadha, we are honoured to have the great Chinese monk in our midst.'

One of Fa-hsien's assistants bowed in return, 'Thank you, oh most magnificent and bravest of kings. The great monk is indeed happy you were able to grant him an audience at such short notice.'

The king accepted his greeting, 'We are honoured by your presence. And we hope you will accept our hospitality.' He gestured to the monk to be seated. A few moments later, it was Fa-hsien's turn to respond to the king, but as he tried to rise to his feet, he slumped forward, falling forward on the cushions, and there was a collective gasp. As his assistants rushed to help him, one of them looked up, and a malicious look appeared in his eyes, as he spotted Atisa and Lila, seated in the front row of the audience. But with a calm face and measured words, Fa-hsien's assistant addressed the king, 'My lord, I regret to inform you, but your generosity has been taken advantage of, and fie upon those who dare. But there are imposters here. We were warned about them too, visitors who threaten the peace of your kingdom. In fact, they might know a thing or two about those who are missing.' His words were met with a stunned silence. He looked around in satisfaction, glad of the effect he had produced. The king stroked his chin, his face giving nothing away before he raised his eyes. He was looking in the direction where the monk's assistant had pointed. But Atisa knew they couldn't raise the alarm, and the king smiled as he caught Varahamihira's eye. Apart from the three of them in the assembly, Atisa was certain, no one knew about Kalidasa's whereabouts yet, and explaining it at this moment would give way to too many complications. The king's reassuring smile hardly helped, for Varahamihira's face had turned red with anger as the assistant's words sank in. 'The young man here is my guest,' the astronomer said, bowing in the king's direction, 'and he is going to assist me in my preparations.'

The king nodded, 'He shall be made most welcome. But you must appreciate, great scientist, that terrible things have happened. And we must take every precaution.' Then turning to the monk, who had by now recovered and was sipping water from a raised pitcher, he said, 'Oh great monk, we understand your concerns.' 'But things don't look good,' Lila whispered. Her father nodded. There was an expression of grave concern on his face. Someone else among the courtiers was standing up. 'If I may, your majesty, we may be safe here and are protected by our loyal guards around us, but there has still been a murder and a disappearance not accounted for.' 'Amarasinha is right,' said another, 'Ghatakapura wasn't attacked by bandits on his way to Deogarh. In your kingdom, thanks to your presence, there are none. But it was a more devious killing, to expose our deepest fears. Ergo, evil should be stopped from afar, before it runs a risk of causing more destruction and more evil. Don't cut off a tree by hacking off its roots, because then it would be noticeable. But to do so by cutting off its water supply, or removing it from sunlight, would be far more potent. It wouldn't be black magic, but something quite like it.'

Varahamihira rose in the splintered silence of the court. He made quite a towering presence, and the murmurs subsided on their own. 'It is true, we have to be very cautious. But we are letting our fears rule us completely. It does not behove us as the king's trusted nobles and advisers.'

There were angry protests at this. The king Vikramaditya followed all this intently, and as he rose to speak and calm down the agitated audience, all the nobles bowed respectfully to him. 'You are a man of reason, oh great Varahamihira, and we respect you for this. But there are questions that have so far not found any answer. Where is Kalidasa? Who killed Ghatakapura?'

The king's face darkened. Atisa knew that the dead man was one of his most treasured gems. He was a magnificent architect and sculptor, who had been the chief designer of the temple at Deogarh, and he had been killed just before it was completed. 'Isn't that true?' asked the king, and the quiet in his tone sounded ominous. His stillness, Atisa knew, was totally deceptive. No one knew how he had sneaked into the camp of the Saka king, and it was much later that the enemy king had been found, dead in his tent. Vikramaditya had done it all very quietly and stealthily. Later, only a letter promising dire retribution if the Sakas continued with their intrusions was found, giving a dire warning. The temple at Deogarh had been a dream project of the king's father, the equally illustrious Samudragupta. Dedicated to the goddess Durga, it promised to be a marvel of architecture, something to rival the stupas of Ashoka or the paintings deep in a cave at Ajanta that the king had once seen in the forests of the west.

'The plans for the temple that Ghatakapura had,' said the king now, his voice measured, and coming from a long way off, 'have been lost too.' 'My lord, let no one's presence here be taken for granted,' someone rose, and his eyes were fixed on Atisa. Something about his face told Atisa he had to remember something. He had not seen this man before, but he felt he had seen him somewhere – a face in black and white – and then he saw the paper fluttering before his eyes, and the portrait Nurah had handed over came sharply to mind. Of course, this one had to be the attacker. The man with the long, narrow face and the scar on his right cheek, who had followed his mother – the one who, as Gaea had reported, had done so with wings on. The whispers around him also mentioned the name clearly, and Atisa knew that he had finally met his nemesis, the man who wanted to kill Kalidasa at all costs and cause infinitely more evil while doing so. He was finally face to face with the man called Dipanna, a great rival of Kalidasa, and who yearned to be among the king's gems too.

'Nothing of that kind,' retorted the king. 'He is the great Varahamihira's assistant, as the great astronomer himself said, and I bid him welcome. For today, there will be no disagreements.' Then he clapped his hands, and the sword fighters rushed in for their performance. They were expert dancers and skilled fighters, and the assembly was soon resounding with their swords, which flashed, moved against other swords and caught the light. All this was done very rhythmically and musically. With the eyes of the crowd riveted on this spectacle, Atisa could not help but glance every now and then at Dipanna. And in one particular moment as two sword fighters rose high against each other, twirling in the light of the lanterns and their shields clashing as they moved in close and then away, he saw Dipanna rise swiftly from his seat and then quickly thread his way towards the doors. He moved backward, facing the assembly, keeping a watchful eye and hoping to give nothing away. Atisa realized Lila had noticed it too, 'I am sure, he is up to something,' she said. 'He's so envious, wants to be one of the Nine Gems. But he isn't just good enough. He is so boring and long drawn.' 'Be careful,' Lila whispered, and he read the worry in her eyes and nodded. 'I won't be late,' and eased himself away, muttering his apologies to those he brushed past, but they really weren't bothered, for the sword fighters' act had them all mesmerized. Everyone looked on with rapt attention; the sword fighters indeed had the audience transfixed. They held tapers of fire in their mouths, and they jumped gracefully with swords in their hand. The flash of their swords streaked across the room like lightning every time their blades caught the light of the tapers, and it seemed as if the stars themselves were dancing on the ground. The sword fighters moved to a certain rhythm, dancing and moving with an effortless grace. Their carefully coordinated moves, the music of the swords, the swirling flames, the jingling of their anklets and their cries, all made for a hypnotic effect. Amid this, Atisa managed to slip away, careful to keep Dipanna in sight. Dipanna had a blue turban on, and he moved nimbly among the crowds that had collected outside, peeking in through the high arches and fences. He swivelled his way around them, and Atisa did too. He skirted the courtyard, walked the corridors, sometimes walking along the ledges because the crowds thronged everywhere, trying to get into the assembly halls. Everywhere there were performances going on, and some people glared as Atisa pushed his way through. Sometimes he would offer his excuses, but people didn't evince the least curiosity about him. He realized that there were people in the crowds who came from all over. Each group was dressed differently from the other. Some had feathered small crowns, others wore low hats, still others wore deerskin robes, and some groups of sages held tridents and were smeared with ash. Atisa, dressed in his jeans and a loose shirt, and with a bandanna around his shoulder-length hair, didn't stand out in any way. As he made his way through and heard them talking in several tongues, his decoder was suddenly alive with voices from all over. He passed masked dancers, strangely dressed magicians, even some who looked like ghouls, and a group of dancers who were dressed like birds. Their feathers brushed his face as he walked past, and he felt the glitter rub off against his skin, and then someone slipped him a mask, and unrecognized he could walk faster now. Soon he was just a few steps behind the blue-turbaned man, who despite all the care he took, had no idea of Atisa's presence just a few paces behind, amid the crowd. Atisa was walking past a group, when something in their conversation drew his attention. 'These wings can actually make me fly,' said a girl. It was one of the bird people, performers who could mimic birds expertly. A man who had fitted himself with a red parrot beak emitted a mock squeak. 'Really, don't even try that.' 'I mean it, just see this pair. The magician Vetalabhatta dipped it in a magic potion, and he said these wings could help me hop, jump, leap... till as long as the potion worked...'

'But not fly, right? And so that's as much as we can do.' The girl looked disappointed. 'But we could try and add it to our performance before the king. It'd impress...'

'Nothing doing, girl. We don't want to embarrass ourselves. All this needs practice, with or without the help of a magic potion.'

She looked forlorn at the reprimand, and the older man patted her, 'It's all right, once this performance is over, we will go to the great Vetalabhatta and ask for his potion.' And this was where Atisa butted in, 'I could sort of test it for you. Not now, not here,' he said quickly, for he saw the alarmed look on their faces, 'but I do need...'

'Are you from here or...?'

Before the man could finish, the girl handed over another pair of wings to Atisa, 'We know who you are.' She exchanged a quick look with the older man, evidently her father. 'Yes, of course,' he said, following the girl's cue, 'We saw you with your flying machine and Lila. If these wings can help you in any way, please go ahead.'

As Atisa left, folding the wings up carefully, the man said in more hushed tones, 'We hope you are able to find Kalidasa. We hope he is all right.'

He heard the last burst of applause dying away and an encore as the sword fighters took their bows. Then a man who had the loudest possible voice clapped his hands and called for attention. First there was the loud beating of drums, and as silence fell, Atisa could still hear behind him, the flurry of feathers, the odd whisper, and not too far away, he spotted the stealthy way in which Dipanna climbed the walls effortlessly, how he stepped on a twig and then bounded across in a trice across yards of empty space. Meanwhile, in the square, one of the king's nobles prepared to make the announcement. He fixed his turban, ran important fingers over his moustache and cleared his throat. It was obvious he wanted to commemorate this moment to himself by stretching it as far as possible. The people around him waited, and Atisa sensed the growing impatience. Someone stamped his foot, another whistled and then from the back, someone hollered, 'Speak up, won't you? The night will soon be upon us.' The noble looked up and blinked. The drums thudded once more, and a soldier called for quiet and raised his spear high. The noble, who looked nervous at the heckling, now smiled self-importantly and began. *On behalf of the great king Vikramaditya, it is my fortune to tell you that there is news of the great poet Kalidasa. He is safe and alive but unwell.* A murmur went through the crowd, and there broke out a loud cheering and some open weeping. Many looked up with a prayer on their lips. Barely had this died away, when the murmurs of discontent could be openly heard. *That is not true. That he is unwell. That he may have been kidnapped by the Sakas. Yes, and the king doesn't want it to be known.*

Really, yes, and the king has sent his soldiers and spies out, and there is no news. Even the great magician Vetalabhatta hasn't been able to find out, and Varahamihira...

This time it was Atisa, who answered back loudly in Varahamihira's defence. 'But he isn't really a policeman or a soldier. He is a scientist and astronomer. He has to solve the complexities of the universe, not things the police should be solving.' The man who had spoken looked embarrassed now, and a woman next to him piped up, 'It's the eclipse, that's what Vetalabhatta warned about. That it can cause more evil than we can think of...'

Shh...

Everyone in the audience turned to look at them, but a quiet fell as the soldiers raised their spears and the noble called for silence again. 'You dare disbelieve the king's words!'

The silence stretched and looking pleased at that, the announcer went on, with his hands still raised as he pleaded for attention, 'But in Kalidasa's honour, since he is without doubt the greatest of the gems in our great king's court, we will present scenes of his wonderful play *Shakuntala.*'

There were cries of delight, sounds that followed Atisa as he moved into the shadows, creeping into the darkness. The man he followed moved on ahead, looking back every now and then. Atisa moved quietly along the walls, knowing he mustn't be seen. He slipped on the wings, fixing their strings around his wrists and shoulders. He had seen Dipanna head towards the stables, and his steps quickened. He felt the air surge into his wings, and in no time, he felt the power seep into his wings as he jumped on to the window ledges, and found himself zipping along staircases and gliding over terraces. He realized that the wings were indeed magical. In barely a few seconds, he found himself near the stables, with Dipanna only a few steps ahead. Then perched on an overhead branch, Atisa could overhear clearly the scuffle between him and a stable hand.

'You cannot take the horses... I have the king's orders.' 'It is an urgent work, you dolt, and on behalf of the king,' said Dipanna, menacingly. 'Do you know who I am? I must be off soon... and the king has announced a reward for Kalidasa.' 'The horses cannot leave the city...,' the stable hand persisted.

'Who is taking them out of the city, you idiot? I wanted one to ride out in the city. The magic is wearing out from my own wings.' There was a short, abrupt cry, and Atisa knew that Dipanna had struck the stable hand. He had nails in his gloves, and these could have a deadly impact. The boy fell to the ground, and Dipanna rushed in. From his vantage point on the tree, Atisa could see that the stable hand was a bit dazed but altogether not too badly hurt. Dipanna rode off on the horse, and Atisa followed him. He was glad of the wings; the flying machine, for all its powers, would have drawn attention. As the wings fluffed up again, Atisa found himself suddenly light headed, his feet felt weightless and he was rising, higher and still higher. He held out a foot to balance himself, the wings fluttered out and he landed on a window ledge. He was moving none too quietly and was awkward in his movements and so was glad that most people were at the performances. The city was quiet, and it was easy negotiating the streets and the buildings on his own. He flew, leapt and jumped at a faster pace now, keeping Dipanna in view and found the wings had now taken on some extra force. He could float up trees and swing across branches, and he found himself effortlessly sprinting across terraces. He could leap down with no effort, fly over streets and easily jump over the narrow spaces between houses, all with the help of his wings. And he could still see the man on his horse not too far ahead. Soon the streets were darker and narrower. Now he recognized Dipanna only from the sounds of his horse. He was travelling way out of the city, and it made Atisa anxious. Did he know where Kalidasa was being hidden?

Then he too found himself in the forests right on the city's outskirts. He breezed past a few huts, shooed away a few dogs that came barking up, far too curious, and then he heard the scrunching of something underfoot as the horse cantered on, not too far away. Looking down as he swung from tree to tree, he first saw bony remains scattered carelessly and far too randomly. There were also some abandoned pots and pans and low-lying fires, around which mangy dogs still roamed, and instantly Atisa guessed that he was in a graveyard of some sort. From the few fires that burnt still, smoke arose, and there was something in the air that even seemed to scare Dipanna's horse. It neighed nervously, almost plaintively, refusing to go forward, and Dipanna thwacked it viciously and repeatedly. Atisa raised his arms and felt his wings stretch themselves again to their fullest extent, and once again, he was moving among the trees, with their thick low-hanging branches that hid him very effectively. There was but one anxious moment, when a branch creaked, and Dipanna paused, but his horse was skittish. It shrieked again very shrilly, and Dipanna struck it again and they were off, the thudding of hooves mingling with the moving branches and drowning out everything else. Sometimes Atisa found himself directly over the low-burning fires, and it made his eyes water. He knew then that Dipanna was there for a purpose, perhaps to meet someone. Atisa slowed down and lingered in the branches. A pair of squawking crows fell silent as he neared and then eyed him curiously. Dipanna had slowed down, his horse still bounced and he cursed under his breath. Then he almost shrieked when a hooded and cloaked figure rose from amid the stones and discarded bones piled in a heap, next to a fire slowly dying out. To Atisa, it looked like a floating apparition that had appeared from nowhere, but he realized that it was someone who was nervous and evidently trembling at Dipanna's approach.

The taper the figure held up fell, and his hood slipped as he bent to lift it. Dipanna dismounted far too quickly and reached for the torch instead. At this, his horse, already frightened, shied and bolted, running away with some relief into the darkness of the trees beyond. The sound of its hooves hammering away mingled with the trembling man's sighs.

Please let me be, please. 'It's too late for that, isn't it?' Dipanna snarled, 'You had the need to show off your new medicines that could make a man sleepy and forgetful, even of things he is sure about. Didn't I tell you I wanted more, and that the great monk should die before reaching the court? But you think once the king knows what you did, he will let you go?'He laughed so evilly that it made the gooseflesh rise on Atisa's arms. It was a cackle that made even the leaves freeze. The sparrows chirped in great agitation and the crows flew off, shaking the tree Atisa was perched on.

'You are in my power, in every way, oh great magician, Vetalabhatta.' The name made Atisa pause. He had heard the name too many times already. He remembered the bird performers and their mention of his magic potion that would make someone with wings fly. The other man tottered to his feet but fell again, and Dipanna cursed, 'You sick, weak man… get up, you have nowhere to hide, except where I tell you.'

The man fell at his feet. He had turned to jelly. He cried piteously, and Dipanna lifted him to his feet. 'Now go and get the monk. What will the world think when they see the great

Vetalabhatta grovelling at my feet, taking my orders. For he will now prepare a medicine that will make the great Chinese pilgrim go stark, raving mad, delirious and even demented till no one believes he still has the wisdom that made him so sought after... and what is more, he will deliver it to Fa-hsien himself.' Atisa shivered for the man who now grovelled at Dipanna's feet, pleading for mercy. 'Please don't make me do this. I would rather forget all my skills.' Dipanna spoke in a voice full of rage and contempt, 'You will do nothing of the kind. You will be in my power long years from now. Remember Kalidasa, and never ever forget.'

The menace in his voice made Atisa shiver. The branch he waited on moved in an agonizingly slow manner, and for an anxious moment he thought he was seen, but the smoke was thick everywhere. It swirled thick below, encircling the trees slowly and almost deliberately, even the one he was hiding in. He realized that Vetalabhatta was being blackmailed very effectively and smoothly. The magician was accused of supplying medicine to Kalidasa, and it was his potions that had made Fa-hsien sleepy. Vetalabhatta was aghast, 'You rogue, you said the medicine wasn't for him, for Kalidasa, but for your sick uncle.' Dipanna laughed, in the way he had done earlier, 'Oh but we do know what happened don't we? What made the poet vanish? What is making him stay in hiding still?'

Then almost to himself, though Atisa could hear him clearly, Dipanna said, 'But not for long, never for too long.' 'It was you, not me, who gave it to Kalidasa, all under a false pretext, and now you want me...,' said Vetalabhatta, and then yelped as Dipanna struck him with force. 'Yes, but the medicine was meant for him, and everyone knows only you can make it...'

The wind sighed through the trees; somewhere a piece of kindling rolled over and crackled as it caught fire, and in the midst of this, Atisa heard Vetalabhatta's muted sniffles. Dipanna said, 'Now we've managed to indispose Fa-hsien, but we need him dead. The king will then be sure that none of his vaunted Nine Gems can do a thing. And I will be one of them. The one that survives...'

'You are nothing but a rogue,' Vetalabhatta hissed. The sound of Dipanna striking Vetalabhatta with his whip echoed and lingered, as the birds once more scattered in alarm. The magician groaned and fell to the ground again. It was terrible to hear him. Dipanna bent down, 'So tell me, do you have it? And are you going to do it, or shall I?'

As Vetalabhatta wailed in renewed misery, Dipanna swooped down and snatched a vial. He held it up and chuckled again, the evil sound making the wings on Atisa's shoulders stiffen and creak. The vial caught the firelight, and he saw a fiery purple liquid swirling inside. 'And so now I am off to... you-know-where. This time I shall make no mistake. I will get him, you know who I mean – get him forever – and I shall be the greatest poet this world has ever seen. Meanwhile, you prove yourself to be the great magician that you are and head instantly to the lodge where Fa-hsien is...'And before long, he was away, plunging into the darkness. He had gone so swiftly that only the branches of trees moving back to their original shape showed the sign of someone having rushed hurriedly past, only moments before. Through the gap that appeared, he saw Dipanna spread his arms and the wings appeared in no time. Perhaps Dipanna had been strapped to them all this time. Atisa was now torn between following him and the urgent need to warn Fa-hsien. A glance down soon decided matters. The light from Dipanna's wings had vanished, and Atisa could no longer tell where he was. Atisa descended to where Vetalabhatta was making his own tortuous way forward. He was limping and dragging his right foot behind him. Then he stopped, poured something over himself and the next moment, there was a magical transformation. Atisa looked on and saw how Vetalabhatta now set off at a fast pace, helped by all the magic he knew, despite his limping right foot. It all presented a very odd effect. It looked as if he was skating, the end of his long robe stretching behind him. Atisa turned swiftly around when he heard the sound of horse hooves and found that the stable hand had caught up with him. He felt something fall flat against his arms, and the wings lay limp and flabby against his skin; they felt papery. While Dipanna's wings seemed to work, the potion on his had worn off. The stable hand's eyes widened, 'I know who that is. You must rush fast. That is the magician Vetalabhatta, and he will run as fast as lightning. We were always a bit afraid of him. We kept away from him – he used to collect stuff from the graveyards and cemeteries. And we left him alone...'

He got off and held out the reins to Atisa, 'Take the horse, quick.' Atisa had no time to thank the stable hand. He knew he had to rush, and with a hurried word of gratitude, he swung himself up on to the saddle and caught up with the magician soon. Vetalabhatta turned, and his injured right foot threw him off balance. He looked at Atisa with piteous eyes, and then as if he knew why Atisa was following him, began speaking in a trembling voice. 'I know why you are here. But let me go. I have to see this through.' Atisa made to speak, but the man held his hand up, and this time he saw his gestures were steady. His eyes moved wildly, as if to keep pace with his thoughts, and when he spoke, his words tumbled out as if he had no time to spare. 'No, I have to. And it's not what you think. No harm shall happen to Fa-hsien; instead, the world shall know the evil Dipanna is capable of. His hatred of Kalidasa will make him do almost anything. So let me go.' He was so insistent that Atisa had to relent. 'I do hope you are careful.'

Vetalabhatta waved reassuringly and was once again making his way through the trees. When his leg caught against a tree, the tree bent with a frightful creaking noise and then righted itself of its own accord. Vetalabhatta extricated himself with no great effort, and looking on, Atisa could only gasp. He had seen for himself some of Vetalabhatta's magical prowess. He was making quick progress, and Atisa had lost sight of him in no time. It was surprising the way people vanished so fast. His horse, a sturdy and strong animal, found it hard to keep up. All around him, he again heard the sound of horses. The soldiers were out again on their patrol. In the heightened, tense atmosphere, Atisa didn't want to be sighted. He knew that with no proper papers, he could well be stopped and even apprehended.

At the Monastery

Fa-hsien had been lodged at a monastery at the far end of the city. It had been built by a wealthy merchant and was furnished with every comfort. The king Vikramaditya himself often used it as a getaway or whenever he wanted to experience for himself the serenity offered by its beautiful gardens. The moon was a thin sliver now, hidden by clouds, and Atisa was glad of the faint darkness. It would help him remain unseen. Barely a few days remained now for the great eclipse. He left his horse by the stables and was glad when one of the stable hands smiled in recognition. 'We know this horse, he is from the palace. You must be known to Govind.' 'Yes,' panted Atisa, 'and I am in a rush.' He had to know where the monk was. Despite Vetalabhatta's assurances, he knew he could not put anything past Dipanna. The stable hand grinned as he saw how worried he looked. He pointed a bit too casually for Atisa's liking to the garden. 'He's taking a walk now, having slept the afternoon off. He wanted some fresh air.' Atisa walked through a high arched door, with gargoyles looking down at him. He ran down the entire length of a long corridor; its windows allowed him a view of the garden, but Fa-hsien was nowhere in sight. Finally, he saw him by a lotus pond, looking morosely at its depths, with his attendants looking anxiously on. At that very moment, there was a rustling in the bushes, and he spotted in the foliage the skulking figure of Vetalabhatta. Atisa knew that however benign he professed to be about his intentions, he had to warn the monk about the magician, and so he leapt out of the open windows and dashed towards the pond, the dew grazing his boots and the grass crunching under his soles. One of the monks turned to him in alarm, and Atisa raised his hand in reassurance, hoping he wouldn't be stopped. He knew Vetalabhatta was a desperate man, trying to make amends for the wrong he had unknowingly done. Dipanna's threats and his own fear were egging him on and making him reckless. He would stop at nothing in his own way just as Dipanna too wouldn't. Vetalabhatta had moved into the bushes, sensing Atisa's presence, but a mere rustling gave him away. He was nevertheless slowly but surely moving forward. Looking past the monk, Atisa saw to his amazement how quickly Vetalabhatta was able to change himself. Sometimes he could be small enough to skulk behind a flowerpot, or he could narrow himself to hide behind one of the tall pillars in the courtyard, and in this manner, slowly and surely he was inching towards Fa-hsien. Atisa could delay matters no more. As he emerged, heading for the monk, some of his acolytes held their prayer beads high. These appeared to spread a gentle white glow around, but it was a white that didn't ebb and falter. Instead, Atisa felt it spread, lighting up the grey dusk in strange blue and purple patches, and then he saw Vetalabhatta clearly. He had opened a vial up, and having resumed his normal shape, was now rushing out from behind the bushes. The halo of light spread, and it threw sparks that died down, only to give way to sudden gusts of wind, and everything swirled, heaved and dashed up and down. The wind thumped on the roof, it clamped hard down on him; it made everyone cough and lie face down on the ground.

The wind howled through the open windows, the leaves scrambled across the yard and over the roof, and when there was a lull, he could hear the frightened screams around. He heard the patter of running feet, the sound of doors slamming shut and the wind picking up speed all over again, rising and shrieking, dying down only to pick up moments later. He tried to move forward but couldn't. He realized he was trapped on the terrace and that was amazing, for he wondered how he had managed that. He shivered, as the wind swelled around him like a thousand escaped spirits that were calling out to him, drumming on the roof, playing with the trees as if all these were musical instruments of some kind. When it stopped all too suddenly, he couldn't believe it. But the silence stretched, the breeze now blew gently and he took his first hesitant steps forward. Apart from a few bruises and scratches, he was all right. Then looking down, he heard the shouts as people gathered around, their low murmurs and then the stern commands of soldiers evidently trying to keep order. He walked down the stairs cautiously, still unsteady on his feet and noticed Vetalabhatta lying face down, moaning to himself, the vial in his hand open and the strange smoke still escaping from it. There was a blue flame around the lid that swayed and heaved; it seemed to be dancing to a faint musical intonation that reached Atisa in a high-pitched singsong chant. *Stay away,* one of the soldiers who had quickly appeared, ordered. He lowered his voice as he took in Atisa and instantly recognized him. 'I know you. You are the pundit's assistant.' Atisa then knew that despite Varahamihira's extreme dislike for the epithet, that is how he was known. He looked down at the man prostrate on the ground and felt sorry. Vetalabhatta had been trapped by his own power. The potion had let loose a storm, and he too had been caught in it. It threw him up in the air and flung him down, none too gently. His injured right foot now lay in an awkward angle. It was obvious he needed medical attention, and quickly. 'We must get help,' said the soldier, 'for the great monk. And for the magician too. We must.' In a darker tone, he added, 'His magic obviously won't help us this time.' Atisa inhaled the strange smell emanating from the bottle. While it had lost much of its potency, it still had a heady, sweet fragrance. He went near Vetalabhatta and sensed that he was trying to say something. Atisa caught his slow murmur, as he spoke up with the last ounce of strength in him. Atisa saw a cloud of blue and purple smoke appear from his lips, and it vanished just as quickly. 'You must get hold of Dhanvantri, the physician. Only he can help the monk in time.'

Atisa patted him, as Vetalabhatta's head dropped back into the grass. Fa-hsien had already been rushed away by his disciples. 'The monks are a brave lot,' said the soldier, who had overheard the magician's words. 'A horseman has already been alerted, and they have rushed to the king's court to fetch Dhanvantri, but...,' the commander bowed apologetically, 'something faster would have been always welcome.' Atisa wished now he had his flying machine with him, but he hadn't had time to even repair it. Even his wings, now devoid of all magical potion, were of no use. Vetalabhatta twitched and shivered, and more smoke escaped out of the vial. 'Be careful,' someone shouted. Before anyone could do anything, Vetalabhatta had bitten down hard on it, and it was only after a minor scuffle that they could prise it out of his mouth. He mumbled through his lips, which were slowly turning black, and his words were hoarse and thick, 'Please save the great monk first. I had to do what I did, to save my own honour. I fell into Dipanna's trap. First he told me he needed a potion for his uncle, and then he blackmailed me.' Atisa shook his head sadly, 'But you couldn't help showing off, could you?'

There were tears now in Vetalabhatta's eyes, and his voice faltered as he spoke. 'It was the best I have ever created, and its secret shall die now. I will never create potions like it again.'

He thought Vetalabhatta would say no more, but he spoke up once more, summoning up all his strength, 'Save Fa-hsien quickly. Dhanvantri has the antidote, and Dipanna needs to be stopped. He will stop at nothing now.' Vetalabhatta laughed incoherently, his speech slurred now, 'But I've given him a medicine that will make him forget. It will make him go wild in the forests, and he will lose all memory.' After that, he fell into a dead faint.

At the Palace

As Vetalabhatta was lifted and taken away to be tended to by the monks, Atisa knew he should return too. It was a long ride back, and from a great distance away, he heard the announcement from the palace at Pataliputra. First the drummers beat their drums in the usual way, and then a voice rang out, loud and clear, carrying far in the breeze.

At midnight the next day, all lights would go off. It'd be a special day of prayers. All people were to repose faith in the king. Sinister enemies were out to harm the kingdom, but the great king Vikramaditya had battled the best of enemies and emerged unscathed.

Atisa rode fast, urging his horse onward. He bent down, his face against the horse's neck. When he looked up, he saw he was passing through the same forests he had been in a while ago. And this time, he saw the lantern flickering through the trees. Its unexpected appearance surprised him. Its light dwindled and almost vanished before appearing again. Sometimes it seemed farther away than he thought it was. Someone was running hard, and the lantern soon died out. The thought that it could be Dina, the pathfinder, crossed his mind and he hoped all was well.

A while later, the sound of the beating drums soon gave way to the tramping of elephants. He heard the heavy rustling of branches and the prolonged trumpeting of the animals as they pushed their way through. Soon their snorting and loud breathing was upon him, but Atisa could still hear from a long way off, the sound of someone running hard, before he was swallowed up by the dense forest.

It was then that he spotted Nurah emerge from the nearest copse of tress. He grinned good-naturedly on seeing Atisa and began playing on his harmonica. It made quaint elephant noises, and Atisa realized that he was signalling the animals to fall in line, once they emerged from behind him. He smiled in return, but it was impossible to carry on a conversation with Nurah, for all was drowned as the elephants picked up pace in the forests. They ran fast and furiously, Atisa following as best as he could. He felt the rush of air all around him and the loud thrashing of branches as the elephants went relentlessly forward, and so he had little idea when all this gave way to the most unexpected storm. The wind first tore through the trees. Strong gusts bent and twisted the trees cruelly, leaving behind shaking branches in their wake. The wind even whipped the clouds above into a frenzy. Thick, dense, blue-black clouds tossed and lapped against each other, and powdery fluffs broke out and fell on them too. Atisa looked bemusedly at Nurah – there had just been one storm too many. No wonder people were jittery. Nurah though only fixed his cap more securely on his head and winked at Atisa, who said, 'We have to get to Pataliputra soon. Heaven knows what Dipanna would be up to. It's time to warn everyone about him.'

'Don't worry,' Nurah replied, 'news must have got around by now. As for us, we mustn't make a scene of our arrival in Pataliputra. Things could be dangerous.' 'I wish there was a way,' Atisa said, 'to send a message to the physician Dhanvantri.' Atisa was just beginning to get a bit frustrated. There were too many things to think about, at the same time. Elder Lama's advice about taking one thing at a time just wouldn't work. Nurah pointed again, and this time Atisa saw the flash of another lantern clearly. It came from the palace, and its repeated signalling meant that it was Lila trying to signal him. *Wait.*

But just then the clouds came in the way again, and he lost the signals. The wind was everywhere, heaping the clouds into a thick impenetrable mass. 'Someone is on his way already,' Atisa said, looking puzzled, wondering if he had deciphered the message correctly and that it was indeed from Lila. He wished he had his machine. Nurah and the elephants swirled before him. 'Oh dear, fog seems unusual at this time of the year,' said Nurah. As the wind whooshed and drummed in their ears, and the descending clouds whispered around them, Atisa knew Nurah was now just that bit worried. 'There are some who would relate it to the eclipse of the moon, but the great astronomer...,' Nurah's voice broke, and he said again, sounding rueful, 'oh dear me, I've forgotten his name again.' Atisa was urging his horse on now. The wind was fearsome, and as he moved eastwards, he felt the fog clouds thicken around him. Had Lila indeed been trying to tell him that someone was on his way? The wind was pushing them in the opposite direction, and then he felt the first drops of rain, cold and hard on his face. Nurah handed him a telescope, looking nonchalant at Atisa's expression as to how he had managed to procure this. 'Try it, it isn't like anything you've seen.' He gladly put the telescope to his eyes. It was amazing. He could see past the clouds and a long way off. It was far more advanced in many ways than Daedalus' old Greek telescope that was a thousand years old and more. Atisa wanted to check it carefully but didn't want to make Nurah suspicious or hurt him. It could be any modern-day instrument, he thought, as he felt its smooth hard silken surface and the lever that with the gentlest of touches allowed for an effortless zooming. He saw the river far away and the palace walls too, with the king's flag flying high and proudly. For all the confusion around him, the river was still. He could see no boats plying except for a lone long boat, which was speeding along as if in a hurry to reach its destination. Then a few moments later, he saw a movement among the trees, a flitting black shadow on the road, and it was headed towards them.

Lila's message came back to him. *Someone is on his way.* Through his telescope, he saw that whoever was zooming past the trees with an amazing agility had on the same pair of wings that Vetalabhatta had designed.

Atisa saw too that he was on the road that led out of the city, the very route he had taken when heading out from the monastery. Atisa feared it could be Dipanna, alerted by their presence and out to wreak vengeance. The wind grabbed him then, and the reins sprang out of his hands. He was dashing through the clouds, being carried along at a great speed. He could only hold on to the reins, clinging for dear life, but the horse carried him at a pace faster than he could imagine. The sounds of the elephants grew fainter after a while, the forests stilled and though his hands still shook from the speed with which he had been carried, Atisa raised the telescope to his eyes once again. Now he saw the flying man clearly and knew for sure it was someone he had had a glimpse of only the other day at the assembly in King Vikramaditya's court. It was the physician called Dhanvantri, one of the king's Nine Gems. Lila had been right. He was indeed rushing off to treat Fa-hsien at the monastery. The rains eased as Atisa neared the city, but the smoke from the sacrificial fires lay thick and dense everywhere. It was at this point a very still day. The flitting shadow was moving fast. The man he followed seemed to ably evade the guards and the soldiers patrolling the streets, who were ever watchful and wary. They moved in groups as if they were nervous and yet watchful. The light from the flares they

carried moved in dizzying circles, as the soldiers ever alert on
the palace towers, marched in perfect order. Atisa waited for
Nurah and his elephants to catch up with him. They took their
time, and Nurah was his usual apologetic self when like before,
he stepped through the trees, with his elephants behind him, in
an utterly magical way. A moment later, though, the agitated
look was back on his face. Not for the first time, Atisa wondered
how he managed to change expression so very fast. Nurah
shook his head, as if he regretted having forgotten something.
His cloak now rustled as he rummaged for something inside.
'The princess is here. We must get a message across to her.'
But at the imposing, tall gates, heavily bolted with huge iron
bars, the soldiers refused them entry. 'For the next two days,
we are not to allow anyone in. The eclipse is only a day away,
and if the world is destroyed, we must still save our king.'
Nurah persisted. He showed them his seals of identity, but the
guards, loyal to a fault, were unrelenting. One of them said,
'The princess is very sick. She is not seeing anyone.' Nurah
then reluctantly used the last card he had. 'Listen good soldier,
my man here,' pointing to Atisa, 'has something for her.' The
soldiers raised their torches, and as their eyes widened in
recognition, Nurah slipped a hand inside his cloak and pulled
out a manuscript. Atisa recognized it as the one Kalidasa had
been working on in the temple. 'As you can see, the scroll has
the king's seal and Kalidasa's sign,' warned Nurah. Now the
soldiers lowered their spears, and sullenly announcing Atisa's
name several times in stentorian tones, as was the practice,
they lifted the bolts and led him in. He saw the suspicion in the
eyes of every soldier he passed, and he read it in the muffled
footsteps of the palace attendants and the stillness everywhere.
There was an atmosphere of utter caution.

Once he reached the chambers in the palace allotted to
them, Lila welcomed him with a delighted smile. She was

careful not to sound too excited. 'Father was in a meeting. He
has all his scrolls with him. There is a debate between him and
the astrologers.'

The Night Before

Predictions were that it would be the longest eclipse ever witnessed. Already the warnings were out, and clearly conveyed, as announcers took over the main square outside the palace. There was no let-up in the soldiers' patrolling. In the streets, there was no one out. Not even a leaf stirred. From the forests, there were weird noises, and Lila explained very casually, as if she wasn't afraid of them at all, that they were the *kapaliks* or the forest sages who frequented the graveyards and cemeteries. The princess though was still very sick, and they waited anxiously for Dhanvantri to return. But the night only darkened, and everything went black gradually. Atisa saw the fog advancing, moving on from the forests to over the terrace houses, and he saw the flares on the high fort walls turn smoky and grey as it moved still closer. The soldiers only lit more flares in a gesture of reassurance. Feeling restless with nothing to do, Atisa fitted up his flying machine, the balloon cloth still torn in places, and rode through the empty skies. He promised himself he wouldn't fly far, and below he saw clearly dots of light moving in circles around the palace and at the walls of the city. It indicated the constant presence of soldiers, and that was a comforting thought.

His machine was invisible in that dark night, and he flew on, mingling with the night. After a long while, he heard the familiar crackle from his sound catcher, a crackle loud enough to get the attention of the soldiers below. He saw them scanning the skies with raised torches, and because his machine, already weary from a long journey in the past, couldn't really take a hit or several hits from a spear, Atisa thought it best to descend. The extensive terrace of the palace provided a perfect landing ground. He was certain the message was from his father, and it had been ages since he had heard from him. The special transmitter button was on, and Atisa knew he hadn't been wrong in his assumption. His father for his part couldn't wait to get started. 'I've the most extraordinary news. I got a message, rather it was left in my tent, and it's from your mother.' Atisa could hear his father's relieved laughter over the distance. 'Not an email or a message left on my transmitter but a handwritten one, and she's never sent me a love note like that ever.' He paused. Atisa could almost imagine his father's rueful, embarrassed face. 'But I am glad she's safe.'

Atisa too felt a profound sense of relief. His father's gentle laughter rose and mixed in the quiet night. 'I don't know how the note managed to get to me. It is a bit of a surprise. There is always someone in the camp, and the smallest sounds are picked up by my sound catcher here.' Gesar went on to talk about the eclipse, the enthusiasm undiminished from his voice. 'I hope you get to see it, wherever you are. This is the most unusual lunar eclipse. From the Everest, it will present a delightful sight.' 'I have never seen the moon so closely,' he continued excitedly. 'It's huge and golden, and there in the distance is Mars, and it looks redder than I have ever seen it look. I would love to photograph this. The other cameras now work fine, though I still haven't found what I lost and the telescope.' Atisa wished there was a way he could help his father. He leant forward as the last word from his father caught his attention. 'Telescope?'

'Yes, it's just one of those things I can't find.' He couldn't bring himself to tell Gesar about the strange telescope he had seen with Nurah. He couldn't let himself be suspicious when Gesar still sounded very excited. He had to be attentive because every now and then, Gesar's voice would break off, and he would instead hear sounds of the mountains and the clouds far away. 'Tomorrow, Mars will be closer, and the moon too – so close and golden, it will be the most magnificent thing ever. It will be the time I will also fly across to see if can find Gaea…'

This time Atisa broke in, hoping to give him some news too, 'Father, I do have some news. I don't think she is there…'

Then he heard a last crackle. The transmitter attached to the sound catcher spluttered and fell silent. He then turned to hear the tread of feet, and there was someone else on the terrace. Someone who was veiled, and yet with a majestic air, and Atisa knew at once that it was the princess. She stood tall and fair, her veil flying in the breeze. The faint light of the tapers reflected on her golden bangles. She lifted her head to the skies and breathed it all in. Atisa read happiness and relief on her face. 'I've the new secret play that you left for me. So is he here?'

He bowed, in the way he thought one bowed to princesses, and behind her, he heard Lila's stifled giggle. Embarrassed, he said as seriously as he could, 'Yes, your highness, but we must keep him safe, till…'

'Till the man on his trail is caught, you mean; everyone is so fearful already,' finished the princess. 'Oh, but your highness, we had a plan of our own.' This time, Lila stepped out of the shadows, looking apologetically at Atisa for embarrassing him. 'I was hoping to tell the princess that we be allowed to go in your flying machine. It has a lantern, right?' her eyes were shining in the candlelight, 'and it would be interesting to watch the eclipse up from real close.'

Prabhavati laughed, 'You are talking much too fast Lila, and anyway you must wait for the king. Only he can give permissions like that.'

Atisa and Lila exchanged looks of frustration, but there was little else they could do. He had hoped to see the moon from up close, nearer than even his father would.

'I wonder where Nurah has vanished again,' said Lila as everyone retired for the night. The bells clanged for the last time that night in fervent prayer, and conch shells sounded sonorous above it all. Elephants trumpeted, and horses neighed. When the sounds died away, all that remained was the chanting of prayers.

The king was out touring the countryside. It was to reassure and comfort the people who were nervous. Varahamihira was ensconced in his chamber again. He surrounded himself with his scrolls that were soon filled with his neat, meticulous writing. As Lila and Atisa worked in their rooms, they heard the curtains rustle and through the window, the pathfinder stepped in.

'Where have you been?'

'and where's...?'

Atisa and Lila had asked the question at the same time, and Dina looked at one and then the other, a twinkle in his eyes. 'I had to break in, using unusual ways, but it's a dark night and I thought of giving you this.'

From inside his robes, he pulled out something, his movements so fast that when he held open his palm, Atisa and Lila gasped. He held out for them a glittering diamond, almost as big as his thumb. 'Yes, deep in the heart of the mountains, you find these,' he said. 'Our tribe protects these stones. That is why we defend ourselves and our secrets. But this stone, the biggest one ever found, is special to me, and it's mine. It is with this, that I have found my way through many a dark tunnel. And on the eclipse night, the night of total darkness like never before, this stone will light things up for miles around.' 'It is indeed as bright as a small bulb,' said Atisa.

'A what?' asked Lila, with the bewildered look that always made him speechless. There were some things he just could not explain to her. 'You could use it on the lantern,' said Dina, missing her question totally, 'and perhaps you will be safe in this rarest of rare eclipses. I think it's best you have it. While I know my way about, there are those who may target me. This stone has magical properties. The black magicians know about this, which is why stones like this are highly prized. We have tracked down smugglers in our mountains who have crushed stones and swallowed them, hoping they would be restored by a surgeon.' He said it calmly, but there was no mistaking the steely ruthlessness in his tone. 'We have looked after the king and the princess, because they saved us from the Sakas, and so it was our responsibility to look after Kalidasa. He is safe, but I think there is still danger afoot for the empire.' 'He is safe...,' he reiterated, seeing the uncertainty in their eyes. 'That machine of yours,' he looked mischievous now, 'can pick up sounds, I am sure. Listen...'

But what the sound catcher picked up was a sudden whirr in the sky, a blip that rose and fell, and as Atisa rushed to the window, the telescope raised to his eyes, he heard Lila too. 'That is Dhanvantri. He is back. But look, those magic wings are giving way so fast.' It was evident that the wings were not going to hold up the physician for much longer. One wing was already flopping loosely, and the other was moving in an alarmingly slow manner, and it was obvious that Dhanvantri was using his own skills to hold himself up. 'We must get to him fast,' said Dina, for once looking helpless. This time, Atisa couldn't help it. He had to think fast and despite the risks from spears randomly aimed, the physician had to be rescued. The kites fluttered open, rattling and creaking, the bellows pumped in the air and the machine revved up with a loud whooshing sound. He was flying at a low height and the machine fluffing up with a low roar, like it always did, drew attention. There was a gasp and then shrieks of delight and horror. The physician looked up too, but he was noticeably faltering. He was striking the air around him with his bare hands, and as Atisa flew up, wondering how he would reach him when the streets were so narrow, Dhanvantri's arms brushed against a ledge, and he reached out and held on to it for dear life. Atisa looked desperately for a place to wedge his machine in, but the narrow lanes and the houses crowded around each other gave him little chance. His machine would get trapped. Already there were children and people on the streets, roaring in excitement. Atisa worried about causing a serious law-and-order problem. And so he bent down, using his sound decoder to full effect. *Keep away. I am the king's messenger on a special mission.* 'He's a messenger from the moon,' yelled someone. 'Keep away.' The sound catcher was clearly picking up the sounds of their conversation, and Atisa navigated his way over the narrow roads and lanes, dipping low over houses, some with stretched out, extended terraces and others with more uneven rooftops and galleries with friezes. His machine was not really made for moving around in cities, and even cities in the olden times were crowded and unplanned. He bounced unevenly along the terraces. Pulling in the balloon folds in the space afforded to him hindered his progress. He also had to move up, for fear that the kites would graze the roofs or catch on the free-standing idols and the gargoyles that stood high on terraces. These were placed to ward away evil spirits. Dhanvantri could barely see ahead, and Atisa, flying over terraces, set up a storm of his own. Clouds of dried wheat cakes, and pulses and beans placed out on mats to dry, scattered in the wind as the machine flew close. Eddies and whirlpools flew everywhere, danced over roofs, dipped low into streets and danced down again. In some places, he saw the wind had picked up cloth pieces that were drying, and they flew a short distance too, flapping and bubbling in the sky. He perched his machine perilously on the terrace, from where he hoped to reach down and pull Dhanvantri up. He was startled to find that the physician, despite his exhaustion, was smiling. He held up a vial, 'I used up the last reserves to give myself strength. You couldn't have come at a more appropriate time.' He looked on in relief once Dhanvantri had a secure foothold on the low cabin walls. Dhanvantri said, 'You seem to have had pretty many adventures with this thing you have.' His husky whisper came to Atisa as a ragged storm, for the sound catcher was on. Dhanvantri looked with interest at Atisa, noting his hair and everything else, and then he looked his fill at the machine. 'Quite neat.' Atisa smiled. Dhanvantri seemed so very cool, and despite his recent efforts, he wasn't too exhausted. 'I met someone who resembled you.' Atisa stopped, his hands on the wheel, and the machine stumbled for a bit, before it whooshed and rose up again. Below them, parts of the city vanished in the dark shadows. Surely, Dhanvantri meant his mother. Dhanvantri grinned, in the open way he had. 'Vetalabhatta is a friend and I miss him terribly, and he does get things wrong. The wings, once they begin working, don't really slow down. I travelled much farther than I intended and at too fast a pace for my liking. I met her in a monastery, and yes, she had this map with her. A tribesman had drawn it for her as she once made her way past the plateau, and across the river Narmada. It was one of the old treasured maps that only a certain tribe knows about.' He lowered his voice and added, 'She said that the Sakas know about it too.' 'Then the king should be warned…'

'"No…" that's what your mother said. "No." She said, "Some of them want peace. Some of them in fact may even want to be in the king's service."'

Atisa nodded. 'And where's my mother now?' Dhanvantri dipped his hand into the cummerbund tied around his waist and pulled out a map.

'She was headed westwards. There is to be a big fair, a horse fair. And the Sakas are likely to be there. Some of them have knowledge of the ancient routes, lost rivers and the tunnels through the mountains. She was hoping to meet some of them there.'

The machine whooshed up in the air, and below they soon caught sight of Lila with her telescope. 'Don't worry, I managed to hold on,' said Dhanvantri, laughing once they had reached, as Atisa apologized for the bumpy ride. 'And I could tell the princess,' he continued, winking at Atisa, 'that the flight was eventful and turbulent.' 'I am glad my mother got away safely,' said Atisa, and he was suddenly happy. He wished he could get a message across to his father. He was now doubly assured that his mother was safe and had perhaps found something of interest. 'I am, too,' Dhanvantri shrugged. 'In any case, the conflict with the Sakas has gone on long enough.' 'Oh Dhanvantri,' said Lila, coming up, 'there are already people queuing up for you.' The line stretched beyond his house, to the city walls. There were men and women, old and young, some richly dressed in fancy silks, others more ordinarily. Some were sitting down in fatigue for they had been waiting quite a while, and others were holding up babies, some wailing, others sleeping. But all were waiting patiently for the physician to return to his chambers. 'They want special potions to protect themselves. I do not know why they so fear this.' The atmosphere grew sombre. The next day was important in several ways, and plans had to be well set.

At dusk, the lamps were lit. In the towers, the fires were lit early. These would show the king the way back home, for he still had not returned. 'It is the longest day too, can you believe it?' said Varahamihira. 'Yes, it is. A strange conjunction of several events,' agreed Vaaruchi. Atisa's attention drifted away from the conversation between two of the most famous scientists of the time, for he was looking through his telescope absently. And then the sudden yell brought everyone up short. The sound came from a totally unexpected quarter. A quick glance confirmed that it came from the mansion adjacent to the princess's quarters. Atisa knew that was where the library was. For the last few days, it had been largely vacant. Most scholars had kept away, preferring instead to spend their time in prayers. The dimly lit library had made even Varahamihira frown. 'This isn't a good sign at all,' he had said. 'If even men of knowledge give in to fear and superstition, it is obvious why the common man is so afraid... It is the hysteria, the fear, that is making them sick. Dhanvantri is going to have his hands full.'

The library was a two-storey mud-brick structure, and its large windows were protected by bamboo and reed curtains. Aloe vera plants lined both storeys, for these plants were said to scare away snakes, and incense sticks had been placed to keep away insects. The lamps sealed in glass burnt low and threw shadows on the walls. Perhaps Atisa should have been alarmed by the changing shadows on the walls, the way the darkness suddenly shifted on darkened walls to resemble a passing, moving man – except that it wasn't a trick of the light, it was for real. Later, of course, he would blame himself for missing the signs and the sounds. He had been so engrossed in watching the sights unfold around him, and in keeping an eye out for the king, that he had missed what the sound catcher had picked up. Atisa desperately wanted the king to return early. He needed the king's permission to fly up closer to the eclipse. Elder Lama had explained once that every realm had its own laws, laws that existed in the context of the times.

No matter one's greater learning and knowledge, one had to live by the rules. 'Everything in its context, and for that context.' So Atisa strained with his eyes to see if the telescope would reveal any movement in the forests. All he saw was the rhythmic movement of trees rustling, a sign that a small army moved through it. There were other giveaway signs too, like flocks of birds moving in a particular direction and a sudden break in this, or even a bird falling, which could indicate that it had been struck by a soldier's arrow, particularly someone from the king's hunting party. He had also been distracted by the crowds that had collected below in the courtyard. People had gathered and were pointing excitedly at his telescope, prompting Varahamihira to look up from his notes to say wryly, 'They want a look as well. Soon you will have your own chambers and a line of people like the priests and my friend, the physician.'

Amid all this had been the sound, barely discernible, of a quill moving on a palm leaf. It was the sound almost like a cricket moving slowly across paper. Kalidasa had immersed himself in his writing once again. It was the sound catcher that had picked up the sound of a door slamming shut, of a reed curtain somewhere being pushed aside slowly and then the tap of a step. But Atisa missed all this, or even the sudden disappearance of Dina, the pathfinder. That could have alerted him, but by now everyone was used to Dina's sudden exits and his equally unexpected reappearances. But when the scream broke out, it made the sound catcher vibrate for long moments, and Atisa almost dropped the telescope in his hands. 'It's from there,' said Lila, a moment later, as she pointed her own telescope towards the library. Other sounds now crowded into the sound catcher – the slithering sound of someone pulling along something heavy, the dragging of feet, low moans and the soft roll of a quill on mud floor. There was a resounding crash that followed next, of wooden tablets falling over, and the swishing as palm leaves fell in accompaniment. Through a window, as he ran towards the library, Atisa saw the flash as someone went past. The strong lean build of the person suggested it was Dina, and it appeared he was carrying someone by the shoulder. There were suddenly more people on the terrace, and Atisa looked up to see the princess there as well. She had evidently heard something too, and now she stood visibly calm, craning over the terrace. Then becoming impatient, she snatched Lila's telescope to her eyes and pushed it away a moment later, for the people below raised their voices in greeting to the princess. 'Welcome back, oh princess.' A woman cried out, 'We are happy to see you back, oh princess.' 'And you look lovelier than ever,' said another woman, and this time Prabhavati had to smile. She waved back, 'And I have good news for all of you too. Kalidasa is not dead, I have been told.' There was a gasp of disbelief, a short moment of silence before there were claps of joy, and then the trumpeters at the corners blew their instruments before the princess shushed them. 'Remember the king's orders. We must maintain calm.' 'But no fear, oh princess.'

'Yes, we are not to be afraid. It is going to be an unusual phenomenon, one like never before, but we have great masters and friends from near and far,' she nodded gesturing to Atisa, who stood embarrassed by the window as the assembled crowd now showered its applause on him. 'They have come here to study it. So it is not, it is not, I do assure you, not the end of the world. And the king is there, and our soldiers and men are ready to guard against every calamity.' The crowd's attention was riveted on the princess, and no one noticed the warrior Dina emerge, in his usual quiet, smooth, slithering way. His movements were quick, though he was held up by the man he held over his shoulder, whose blood was soaking into his clothes and falling drop by drop into his quiver and on the stone floor. The princess saw him as she turned away from the railings and turned pale.

For a moment, it did seem she was about to faint, but Lila grasped her quickly by the waist, and Amarasinha, one of the Nine Gems, murmured a soft prayer. 'All that you see may not be true. The appearances that seem most certain are not often real.' And almost miraculously, the princess recovered. She straightened, as she thanked Lila, and her gaze was resolute as she turned it to the approaching warrior. In the sound catcher, the faraway sound of scattering feet and the brush of a quill on the mud floor was once again apparent. 'He is safe, oh princess,' said the pathfinder. And as her eyes widened, Dina dropped the injured man to the floor and his blood formed a small puddle, before the other attendants came rushing forward to raise him again. Atisa recognized him at once as Dipanna, and the memory of his evil cackle once again made him shiver. Everyone around him had the same expression of horror and relief. 'Is he dead?'

Now it was Dina's turn to look nervous, 'I hope so.' His voice trembled, 'At least, I stabbed him because he was sure to kill.' He rubbed his forehead, his hands were trembling and he went on, 'It's not that we kill deliberately. Like all warriors, we do this in self-defence or to protect someone else. And his intentions were, and have always been, since I followed him, evil.' Dina told them, in clear and unwavering tones, of how he had followed Dipanna for a long time. 'What makes him more evil is the pretence he is capable of.' Dipanna had finally had information on where Kalidasa had been hidden away and had tried to sneak in and kill him. But the pathfinder had closely shadowed him and had never once let Dipanna out of sight.

'I did think he wasn't above his tricks,' he said. 'I know

his ways. He had pretended to faint so that he could be taken to the king's special hospital where the great poet had been recovering. And so Kalidasa had to be moved to the library, without your knowledge too, your highness. But this man is evil. Too many times he has tried sneaking into our lands, trailing Kalidasa. And people of our tribe love Kalidasa. There has been many an occasion when he has told us his stories and helped us pass difficult times.'

He placed his sword at the princess's feet. 'Your highness, we are your servants and will serve you with our lives.' 'I know,' the princess nodded, smiling in reassurance, 'the time when I was in a rush to get here, someone showed me the secret way...'

'It was a man from our tribe, oh princess,' said Dina, still at the princess's feet. 'Over the years, we travelling people have come in contact with the Sakas. Some are evil and live a life of aggression, but then some among them have learnt too from our ways.'

Dipanna regained consciousness soon after and looked up dazed. He was surrounded by guards and looked at everyone wildly. He snarled, knowing he was trapped, but there was a frighteningly blank look on his face. Atisa understood it was Vetalabhatta's secret potion at work. Dipanna no longer remembered a thing.

Vetalabhatta's words came back to him. The magician had told him of the potion that Dipanna had imbibed on the false belief that it would make him invincible and all-powerful. But it had been made from the bones of hundred-day-old corpses, especially those who had died a violent death. 'It will make him remember things in fits and starts, and then after a while, only a blank cloud will remain where his memory was,' Vetalabhatta had said.

Dipanna's voice came in faint, broken gusts. 'There was

a woman who rescued the one I was chasing. I chased her through the tunnels.' 'Yes,' said Dina, folding his arms sternly and looking down at him, 'that was when you were chasing the great poet. And he got away.' That sent a buzz through the gathered crowd, but Dipanna had fainted again by then. Amarasinha, the noble from the court, who was present too, scratched his head in some bafflement, 'Oh dear, the medicine does have some untoward effect. Maybe he will remember some things in their correct order later?' 'He certainly won't remember the tunnels,' said Dina with some grim satisfaction. 'That is the secret of our tribe. It is the secret place where the old sages made their journeys – tunnels that opened up when the earth cracked, or when rivers moved through mountains and then changed course, leaving a hole in the depths of the earth. In some places, these are lit by...'

His voice dropped away, and he could not complete his words. Atisa knew he was referring to the diamonds, which he wanted to keep a secret for as long as possible. And so smiling at Dina, Atisa said, 'You can bet Nurah knows a thing or two about these paths. It always surprises me how he gets to places so very quickly.'

The Eclipse

There was a loud fanfare, a blaring of trumpets, as the advance guard of the king's hunting party came in. The princess's face lit up even more. 'Father took a long while this time. He will be happy to learn...'

She touched the warrior on the shoulder, who still remained on bended knee before her, 'I will speak to the king. You and your tribe have been of invaluable service.' Then turning to Lila and Atisa, she said, 'and the king will accede to your request, don't worry.' Lila and Atisa exchanged excited glances and looked across the terrace, where the king's hunting party was now clearly visible. There came into view a troop of white and brown horses, and the elephants that made up the rear. The trumpets blared, and the waving, moving cloud of dust slowed down as the party entered the roadway leading to the city, and then the procession settled to a stately crawl. Conch shells blew, drums began beating and cymbals clashed. There seemed to be a frenzy about it, as if in all the noise, everyone's secret fears would vanish as well. The king took his time waving to the crowds as he dismounted. He walked amid the flower petals and sacrosanct water that were showered and sprinkled on him. He walked to the podium and waited for the cheers to subside. 'There is no evil unleashed. My presence here is proof enough. I am no ghost but your king.'

There was laughter, and cheers rang out again. This time they seemed never-ending. 'Tomorrow, life will continue as we know it. You may have your prayers, observe your rituals, and the palace will have a free kitchen and an organized ritual of its own. The blessings of the goddess are with us. And tomorrow, when this is over, we shall resume the building of the temple at Deogarh. Ghatakapura's death shall not be in vain.'

And sweeping up his robes, as his people called his praise enthusiastically once again, he left for his chambers. The message Atisa and Lila had been waiting for came not a moment too late. The shadows were lengthening, lamps burnt at a fiercer glow and the moon had emerged, filling up noticeably one section of the northern sky, as Varahamihira pointed out. Dina entered silently as before. The princess had rewarded him for his services, by appointing him as a special bodyguard. 'I have news. Kalidasa's new play will be ready for the assembly tomorrow.' His expression lightened, but he couldn't keep the tremor out of his voice. As night set in, it was the fear of there being no tomorrow that had gripped him too, this brave warrior of the mountains. 'And the king,' he managed to bring a smile to his face, 'has agreed. You may fly tonight, and he says everyone's good wishes go with you too.'

'We will set off soon,' said Atisa, feeling relieved, his mind on the task ahead. It would be fun to watch the eclipse from a different time period, but he did wish there was a way to record it all. It would make up for his father's loss of cameras. 'I am going with you, of course,' said Lila. 'I can paint it all. It would be a record of sorts.' It was one of the most silent nights he had ever known. It was eight, as the dial on his clock showed, and the streets were empty. The flickering lanterns made their own whispering noises against the wind. Even the sound of the wind in the trees was clear, and temple doors left open allowed the sound of soft chanting of prayers to filter through. In the distant forests, smoke from low fires was visible. 'Those are special prayers being offered by saints and *kapaliks*,' said

Varahamihira. 'Everyone has their own way of keeping evil at bay. It always surprises me how the moon has such alluring and strange properties when it so very far away.'

The spacious terrace of the king's palace gave them enough space to lift off. Atisa worked on the bellows, and the machine glided off the floor and slid smoothly into the skies. And soon, Nurah's kites too had opened up, fluttering as they spread out in the night sky.

'It will take some skill,' he explained, 'to move up, once there is no wind.' Lila had already sat down on the small ledge that ran all around the cabin walls and had begun to paint. Already the moon looked bigger than ever before. He took the main road leading up north to Kannauj. It was all darkness below, the golden moon turned sections of the forest purple and the broad road running through it looked silver. The boats creaked on the shore, and the sound catcher also picked up the sounds of the animals, the baying of wolves, the calling of the birds, the trumpeting of elephants and every once in a while, the roar of tigers.

'Of course it's the animals,' said Lila looking up from her painting. She was fast with her fingers, and in the low lantern light, he could see already what she had drawn – the moon in all its golden splendour over the northern walls of the city of Pataliputra. 'They can sense things far better and in a deeper way than we can. Our senses, the great Ghatakapura used to say, have been dulled by all our thoughts and the stresses and travails of modern-day living.' 'What he said seems so much true even today,' Atisa couldn't help remarking.

'Sometimes truths never change, in my time or yours,' said Lila. There was something in how she said it that confused him. Suddenly he wanted her to stay his friend, in his time and hers too. Not sure what to think, he lifted the telescope to his eyes. *Look, I can see something already.* But in his mind, Elder

Lama's words returned, 'Sometimes greatness can never appear in a certain time or period, and so no one really knows when Lila lived. Her book is what matters, and in the monastery in Myanmar, I am sure I will find copies of her book too.'

He looked down, and there on that road coloured silver in the low moonlight, he saw the procession of monks far in the distance. They held their lamps up high, and if he listened closely, he could hear their slow, sonorous chanting, something that was reassuring and timeless at the same time. They were returning to the capital from the monastery. Fa-hsien too had managed a full recovery.

The machine dipped low and scudded along pulled by the breeze. The moon's light at moments threw a golden glow over the river and the road, and it seemed to diminish gradually as they moved on. And as he lifted the levers, and the wind died away, he saw a tiny part of the moon drop away, ever so slightly, as if someone had nipped it on the right. Beyond in the sky, every other light was fainter. Behind the moon, in a straight line, he saw through his telescope an unblinking red dot, which was Mars. 'Isn't that wonderful?'

'Something never seen, or will,' breathed in Lila, and her eyes had a reddish-yellow glow, 'perhaps not be seen in a thousand years and more.' He went higher. The air around them was still, and there was no hint of moving clouds. He could hear the slow creak of his machine, the wind quiet in the folds, and the sound of Lila sketching. The lantern below burnt faint, like the moon, a shade of gold. It was as they rose higher that the diamond cast its spell, turning the world below a brilliant silver. Perhaps it was a light that appeared reassuring for the monks too. 'I wish,' Lila said, 'there would not be such fear associated with these things. People believe that the moon is being swallowed up by the demon called Rahu, who tried to stealthily drink the nectar that had been churned up.'

Atisa nodded. He knew the story. 'It's the fear that the evil demon stalks the universe that makes people so afraid, numb even to think.' He went on, 'And if they see these drawings, with the moon looking so beautiful and the world's changing light, perhaps they might not be so scared.' From where they were, over the hills, and with the city and the kingdom spread around them, they could see the moon closer than ever before. They were higher than anything miles around, and as Atisa felt the balloon move and shift, it was almost like the earth moved under him. The moon's glow was fading from where they were. The dark spot had grown in size and was a clear blemish. He saw the empty pools of craters, the high-rising crevasses and the vast expanses of golden white that made up the moon's surface. It was a golden white that was dimming, turning grey in parts. *Oh dear,* said Lila in dismay, and he turned. A colour pot that she had been holding had slipped, and it fell, in a sharp, straight line to the earth. 'It's purple,' she said, looking down over the rails. 'A colour I didn't really need, but I hope it doesn't fall on the wrong person or in the wrong place.' 'The demon splashing people purple,' said Atisa, 'that might give people something new to think about.' The wind died away, and there was a stillness. The procession of the monks had halted too. They were by the riverbank, for the road ran by the river, and the moon's reflection appeared on the waters, showing clearly its changing self in the sky, yellow turning dimmer and then grey, and behind it, the planet Mars had vanished utterly. It had moved, as predicted, into a straight line behind the moon. The moon was one quarter gone now. It was a gibbous moon now, and a purple-blue cloud swirled around it. He wondered if his father was seeing the same thing, and if he had had a way to record it. 'There will be people who will travel to the moon, one day, won't they?' said Lila, almost absently.

He looked at her and wondered if he should tell her that it would all happen, in a thousand years and a bit more. There would be the first Apollo mission and others that would follow, and the moon would be tapped for its minerals and water, when demand for it seemed to escalate on the earth – a future just as she hoped, but one ridden by other considerations and needs. 'Yes, they will, of course,' he said. 'They would need to travel in special spacecrafts that would make them pull away from the earth. And then they would need air to breathe, so they would have to carry it in special tanks. They would have to even wear special clothes.' 'Wow!' she said, and he was startled at her use of that exclamation. 'Don't look so surprised, I've heard you use it at times,' she said laughing. 'In fact, what you say is possible. As father says, every generation builds on what the previous one has discovered. My father learnt from his father and grandfather, men who watched the stars and made predictions. And he realized there was a science there, not just blind coincidence. He is teaching what he knows to me, all the fascinating concepts of mathematics and the puzzles that are possible.' The part of the moon now visible to them had turned blue now. Atisa longed to tell her about the book of mathematical puzzles attributed to her that the Elder Lama was now looking for in a monastery at Myanmar.

From below, the chanting grew louder, the boats creaked on shore, and the fires in the distant graveyards and dry lands burnt a notch higher. 'The *kapaliks* are looking for corpses,' said Lila. 'They think it is at this inauspicious moment that evil enters the dead, and it makes them suitable for all their potions and magic ointments.' Her sketches now lined one wall of the machine, and the moon had sliced to less than a quarter now. 'I didn't know how quickly the earth moves, until now.' 'Yes, it's the earth's shadow that makes it possible. That's what father has always believed, and his forefathers too – that the earth is no flat land but a sphere, and it moves. He just keeps some truths to himself.' 'One day,' said Atisa, 'these truths will be self-evident.' He was about to tell her about Copernicus and Galileo and how the latter was forced to recant, and how in the end, it was his truth that prevailed. Just then, his attention was drawn to sounds from below. Apart from the slow-moving red lanterns, he saw moving in quick big leaps, dots of blue lights, through the forests. The lights bounced, shook and moved fast. 'Horses, do you think?' he asked, and Lila barely looked up from her painting. He knew instantly what it was all about. Nurah was riding back fast, this time with his horses, and perhaps they wore beaded, jewelled saddles and the ropes he used to direct and guide them had beads embedded in them too. The moon's silver was dimming now, and everything was still below.

The horses had stopped, and Atisa, turning up the sound catcher, caught the sound of their harsh breathing and the flicking of their tails. He heard too the scudding clouds and a sound he couldn't place. Perhaps it was the moon's sighs, or the moon dust blowing quietly, or whispering. He looked through his telescope and saw the high ridges, mountains of lava, deep craters and seas of moon sand. He saw a small object, perhaps a satellite from a different time, race towards the moon's surface and the flash of a meteor as it sank in moon dust.

'The moon's such a lovely colour,' Lila breathed. 'In fact, I wish I had all the colours to paint it with.' She was leaning over too far, almost as if she wanted to reach out and touch the moon if she could. He opened his mouth to warn her, but he couldn't. They had moved higher, and a cloud swirled past, dancing past the ropes, and his mouth filled with its mist and her face was lost for moments in that cloud. When the cloud passed, he saw it was all purple and grey, and as the earth

moved, ever so slightly, the colours moved too, and against the clouds, it all made for a breathtaking picture. They held their breaths, the sound catcher picking up the low chanting of the monks and the rhythmic trotting of the horses. Everything in the universe seemed to be moving to a secret rhythm of its own. The shadow of the earth passed low over the moon's crater. It lit up one part of the ridge, and the clouds continued their slow scudding in the sky, as the flying machine lolled and drifted in the high wind between earth and sky.

The clouds farthest up changed colour with the moon too. It was turning grey slowly. 'Only a few more moments,' Atisa breathed. And barely had he finished when the moon vanished. It was as if it was totally wiped away from the sky. At the far end of the sky, it seemed that even the angry still dot that was Mars had vanished. It was the darkest of all nights, and almost in unison, the lights below went out. It was amazing. It was as if the moon had been plucked right off from the sky. Everything was still and dark before the temple bells began clanging frenetically, the conch shells blew and the ululations of the women far and near could be heard. It was all a way to ward off the evil spirits. The horses below stopped. The chanting of the monks dropped to a low hum and stopped completely. Then slowly, almost in a measured way, a corner of the moon, golden and yellow, thrust itself into the darkness. The chanting resumed gently, and it was almost timeless in tone. The bells rang in a more relieved fashion, and as the moon reappeared gradually, restored to its original shape and colours, the bells tolled, the lamps were lit again and the monks' sonorous chanting took on a more regular rhythm.

'Father's prediction was accurate to a large extent,' said Lila. They were drifting gently back, the moon was slowly resuming its golden splendour and Lila's paintings made the inside of the flying machine look like a gallery. 'You know he had the almanacs my great-grandfather had. He had written, having studied the stars for a long time, during his long journeys across the land, that one day precisely such an eclipse would occur, and that the angry planet, Mars, would be right in line too. And father had predicted the year and the date, almost to perfection.' 'I hope all of us can return safely.' But the wind had now stilled, and it took some time for Atisa, with Lila helping him work and steer the ropes, to make a gradual descent towards the flat terrace of the palace.

Their return, together with Nurah's horses and the monks, made for a rather crowded procession that was headed towards Pataliputra. The excitement still remained now, and people were thronging the marketplace and the city centre. The acrobats performed, street musicians played robustly and joyfully in every corner, and there were bear performers and snake charmers. There were crowds outside the temple too, ringing the bells, queuing up to worship the gods. The tenseness of the days before had given way to a joyful relief.

Honoured by a King

'The king would like to see you.' A messenger ran up barely had they pulled the machine in and neatly rolled it up, an umbrella like before. It was late, but the nobles and courtiers had assembled in the open. Lamps were lit, but the light of the moon was enough. There was the princess and next to her, Kalidasa, holding in his hand a palm leaf script. The light wasn't bright enough for him to read, but he was leaning forward, his face only inches away from the leaf, and Atisa saw to his surprise that Kalidasa was wearing glasses. 'Something father designed,' said Lila very matter-of-fact, 'and look there is father.' Varahamihira sat with the other nobles and courtiers, and they rose as one as Fa-hsien entered with his retinue.

There was a great fanfare once again, and it seemed never-ending. Fa-hsien walked slowly, followed by his monks, to the seats on the right that had been specially prepared for them. 'We have never had an assembly convened at such a late hour,' said the king, 'but today is an unusual day, with several unusual things happening. Also,' and he turned to the monk, 'I am glad you look much better now.' The monk bowed, 'It all turned out well. The long walk from the monastery turned out to be a blessing in disguise. I happened to see the moon's magnificence and its almost miraculous appearance as I walked here.' 'It was indeed a rare phenomenon,' agreed the king Vikramaditya, 'and your journey here, great monk, proves one thing for sure, that it is not something to be frightened of. Nor does it spell the end of the world. Our great astronomer was right after all. Oh learned souls, we are indeed honoured by your presence.' Varahamihira inclined his head at the king's gracious words. Then the king nodded as he gestured to Atisa and Lila, 'We have an honoured guest with us, someone who was not afraid to fly up to the moon, or well almost there, and Lila, with her lovely drawings. The moon is not scary. It is one of the most beautiful objects we have outside of our earth.'

He waited for the applause to die out before he said, in a considerably lighter tone, 'And I suppose you will tell us if indeed the demon Rahu swallowed the moon? And what did he look like?'

The laughter took time to subside, and soon the king conferred honours on several of them. There was a marigold garland, a silk shawl and last of all, a palm leaf scroll. Atisa opened his and saw something written in elegant Sanskrit script and marked with the king's seal. It showed Vikramaditya fighting a lion with his bare hands. *Oh great flyer and brave warrior,* Atisa read, haltingly.

He had never been addressed this way, and he tried hard to stifle his giggles. Lila caught him in the act and winked. She opened hers too and mouthed the words so only Atisa could hear. *Worthy daughter of an illustrious father, your exploits today have done everyone proud. May every daughter follow in your steps and bring glory to her family and the kingdom she lives in. The king allots you a plot of land, on the eastern banks of the Ganga, tax-free, for the enjoyment of you and your descendants.*

'Good heavens,' she said, 'I haven't even thought of my descendants.' There was a plot of land for him too, Atisa noted, *by the river Ganga, away from the city.* 'Tomorrow,' said one of the lower court officials, 'you can go to the land registrar's office and ask for a formal grant.' 'He means one set in stone, with all the details,' explained Lila. 'You place it on the land, so that it is evident to everyone, especially so that cattle cannot stray and graze on it.'

The long night ended with two speeches. One was a lengthy monologue by Varahamihira that made Lila fidget and whisper in Atisa's ears that she had already heard it, since he had rehearsed it for her. And then to the delight of all, there was the announcement that Kalidasa too would read from his new work, the one he had composed and lost, and that had been restored to him only recently. Varahamihira began by saying that eclipses could be explained rationally. There was a science behind it. The fact that everyone was safe and had enjoyed the spectacle spoke for itself. The angry planet, Mars, had appeared behind the moon, and that was the rarity of the phenomenon. 'It will,' he said looking up, and with a faraway look in his eyes, 'occur again only 1800 years later.'

There was a gasp, and only Atisa grasped in a particularly special way the significance of what that meant. Such a rare eclipse with three celestial bodies in a straight line would happen in his time, an event his father had gone to capture when he had joined the Everest expedition.

'Is that true?'

Even in that atmosphere of cordiality, he could sense the disbelief and suspicion in that question. And he caught the next sentence uttered behind him in a distinctly spiteful way, 'He thinks his science can explain everything.' The hostility was unmistakeable, but looking back, Atisa saw only a sea of rapt, attentive faces, and he really couldn't be sure who had said it. The next moment, his attention was diverted, for there was a rousing cheer from the audience. Kalidasa had taken the stage next. Varahamihira looked distracted. He was flipping over his scrolls as if he had more to say, but knowing that while many things had been sorted out, the time was not yet right for every truth to be made known. He sighed, and looking up, his eyes met Atisa's and he smiled, lifting his hands good-naturedly skywards. 'Truth chooses its moments,' Atisa remembered Elder Lama's words. Varahamihira's family had kept their scrolls carefully hidden. In time, these had been secreted away to remote libraries and out-of-the-way monasteries, just so they were safe. He realized suddenly that was where Nurah had played a particularly helpful role.

Atisa returned from his reverie, as a silence descended, and everyone in the audience held his breath. Kalidasa cleared his throat, smiled shyly as he looked up at the princess and then began reading from his new work. He narrated to a spellbound audience the story of the cloud messenger who carried messages from a princess to her beloved. It was lustily applauded, the audience breaking out into a concert of clapping, and if anyone realized that the context was somehow familiar, no one really let on. It was all translated for Fa-hsien, who, however, was too sleepy towards the end. A palanquin came in the middle of it all to carry him to his quarters. And with that eventful departure, the night too ended. By then, grey streaks of dawn had already smeared the sky.

I should leave, Atisa was thinking, *the next day,* as he looked at his flying machine. He had already been to the land overseer, and his plot of land allowed him enough space and more to spread out his balloon and inspect it carefully. It would be a long journey back, and he had to get every tear carefully mended. As usual, Nurah too had appeared on the scene and had provided him with a needle as big as a lean sword, to patch up a tear made by a straggly branch. 'I brought back a peace message from some of the major Saka groups,' Nurah revealed and then let on more of the gossip. 'Dina will be honoured in a special way. He will be sent back as a special officer of the king.' 'And there will be no more battles?' asked Atisa. 'Yes,' said Nurah, thoughtfully. 'The king also wanted to make you one of his Nine Gems. You know he keenly feels the loss of Ghatakapura, and of course Vetalabhatta, and would like you for several special reasons to make up... the missing gaps.' He winked before he went on, 'And you'd be the youngest.' 'And yes,' said Atisa ruefully, 'still to complete my studies.' 'If the king had his way,' Nurah continued, 'he'd send you to Ujjain or Taxila, one of the universities.' 'You are thinking too far ahead,' Atisa laughed, holding up his hand, 'and I still haven't any news of my mother, for sure.' 'Oh, but she is all right,' said Nurah and then stopped.

They stared at each other in surprise. Atisa had been about to tell him of the message from his father, but his old suspicions about Nurah returned. He did seem to know altogether too much. 'We are special messengers, dear boy,' he told Atisa, grinning now as if he realized his suspicions. 'Some of my tribesmen have special skills, while I have these special instruments too,' and saying that he pulled out the ear trumpet from behind. 'I can hear whispers and furtive conversations in hidden places, so I pick up messages.' 'You are a spy, in some ways.' 'In some special ways.' 'And now if I did not know how very forgetful he is, or that he is indeed fatigued from his long journey, the great monk Fa-hsien has something to tell you.' He fixed his ear trumpet back on and tightened his cloak around himself before he made his last announcement. 'Now I must get going again. The ships from Java will come up to Tamralipti, and I must head eastwards. See the freshness everywhere. Once people's fears are all gone, it's as if the world is created anew.' Then almost casually he said, 'You should leave soon. Here in Pataliputra, things are safe, but out there in Jhansi, there were posters of you, the one showing you with the ear phones on and the strange belt, and your mother.

There are warnings that you are strangers from space, who came with the eclipse, and must be stopped at all costs.' Atisa laughed. Nurah bit into his lips, quelling his own, and looking serious said, 'Superstitions never die really. In every era, we have to fight them.'

The Monk's Revelations

Fa-hsien was strolling in the courtyard, holding on to his prayer beads. An acolyte walked alongside, his head bent respectfully, as he strained to pick up his teacher's words. Atisa hoped he hadn't barged in at an inconvenient time. Fa-hsien looked up, and for a moment, a puzzled expression appeared on his face. Then the acolyte whispered something to him, and his face broke out in a broad smile. 'Yes, of course, you do look so much like her.' Once more, the image of the *daroga* and the posters of his mother on the city walls came to his mind. Fa-hsien, as if he guessed his thoughts, smiled faintly, 'Oh yes, we saw those too, but there is something in my chambers…'

Then laughing, he turned to the acolyte, who rushed away hastily. As he resumed his walk around the courtyard, motioning to Atisa to accompany him, Fa-hsien explained that he had been in Peshawar not too long ago. There he had found an old stupa in whose inner chamber there were embedded the footprints of the Buddha. He closed his eyes momentarily, whispering to himself, 'our great lord'. 'One day there was a blinding thunderstorm, the kind that appears often in that dusty, cold city, and I was separated from my students. You see,' he said ruefully, 'it was no time to be out. I had been warned. So the storm came down with fierce hail, and it seemed to be sweeping up other things too, leaves and stones and even parts of a thatched roof, and soon palm leaves from a nearby school. So I rushed into the small temple, and once inside, I felt safe before I saw...'

'... there was someone there, and she was taking pictures.' He smiled ruefully, 'Of course it was hard to make out anything, and at that time I didn't know anything about... about...'

'Cameras?' Atisa finished, all excited and breathless.

'Yes, and then she wanted to take a picture of me, but I felt too shy. And I told her about this old stupa and how it had been built by sculptors who had been taught by the Greeks. The Greeks are master artistes, and they also learnt about the wonderful teachings of our master. It was a learning that travelled both ways. She listened, and then I asked her if she would teach me to use the camera... and that is how.'

Fa-hsien stopped again, and by this time, the acolyte had returned. 'Here it is, the picture of your mother.' Atisa stared at it in disbelief. It was just like any tourist picture. There was his mother standing amid some ruins. He could see the broken-down pillars, the stretch of walls and the blue sky. Then he remembered something that Fa-hsien had also said, that there had been a thunderstorm and that it was dark inside. Wouldn't that have made taking a picture difficult, even if it was a modern camera?

He turned to ask, but the monk had sped away. It was time for a great religious debate, and he had to make his preparations. That day he had to leave and couldn't delay it any more. It was difficult to say his goodbyes to Lila. 'I wish you'd read my book on mathematical puzzles when it comes out.' 'I promise you, I will.' 'Judging by the wind speed and the distance,' she was now saying, 'it will not take you more than a day, and your machine does set very impressive speeds.' 'I hope,' he said, 'you won't set too difficult puzzles for me.'

'No, no,' she laughed, 'but you must let me make as

powerful a telescope for my father as the one you have. He is very impressed with yours.' 'Indeed I am,' said Varahamihira, when he went to say his goodbyes to him. 'It will help me carry out my experiments. It could also, don't you think, help the army report on anything suspicious?'

'Yes, it can. It can have all those uses, father,' said Lila. 'But perhaps,' and this time the sadness in her voice was palpable, 'the time isn't right?'

'We can still make our notes, can't we?'

And both father and daughter were soon involved in earnest discussion, and Atisa was glad in a poignant way. It was good this farewell ended this way. He wondered where Nurah had got to. But he was nowhere to be seen. And Dina was away, guiding the king and the princess Prabhavati through the mountains, while their armies followed behind. The Saka chieftains had agreed to negotiate, but they had insisted on absolute secrecy. From a long way off, he looked down through his telescope and saw Lila on the terrace, a small figure in her skirt and silk bodice. She was growing faint, and he waved to her and she waved back one last time. She continued waving, and then he realized to his horror that she was leaning far too much over the terrace. It seemed she was pointing out to something. He looked up and saw heavy clouds headed in his direction. He heard the wind before he sensed it. It made a whooshing, whistling noise as it pulled his machine ever upward, and he breathed and sniffed in the damp clouds and found himself increasingly anxious about Lila. He pushed a light piece of cloud aside and looked down through his telescope. And he saw a most amazing and yet scary sight. She was flying on wings and then faltering. She waved to him but then somersaulted and seemed to be falling back. The clouds came in once more, and he couldn't see her. He would, he knew, never see her again.

She would be safe, he told himself. She would be safe. And he wasn't sure if the dampness on his cheeks came from the misty clouds. Elder Lama had said that the old scripts in the monastery's library had her book too, though it was dated much later. No one ever knew when she really lived. And perhaps that was for the best. He had been part of one adventure, but some mysteries may never be solved.

He was flying over the same crevasse he had crossed only some weeks ago, and then the immense stretches of the river Brahmaputra. He was going to reach in a few hours, just as Lila had predicted. He hoped Elder Lama had returned. Now he knew the secrecy of his mission. The monastery in northern Myanmar that had long borne assaults, especially during the second world war, needed rescue. He hoped Lila's book and Varahamihira's treatise had been recovered. Looking down, he saw once again a herd of elephants, and it was the very orderly fashion of their movement that reminded him of Nurah. But it was evening now, and he knew that the more he travelled eastwards, the earlier darkness would set in. Then a little while later, he saw the flickering lights in his house and a few lamps on at the monastery next door. He burst into his father's study, wondering if his mother had reached, and he stopped short in surprise. For his mother was indeed back, and she had her ear against the transmitter.

She rose to hug Atisa and smiled, 'You always seem taller whenever you return from your travels.' While he said, hugging her back, 'You are wearing the same clothes as you were in the photo.' She looked puzzled and then pointed to the transmitter. 'I am waiting for your father. There has been heavy snowfall and a storm, so his return has been held up. He will fly back tomorrow.' Much later, she asked him, the curiosity apparent in her voice, 'What was this photo you were talking about?'

'There was Fa-hsien, who said...'

'Fa-hsien, you must start at the beginning,' she said laughing. 'I was at that monastery, and there were visitors from all over the place.' 'You mean, you don't know about this photo,' said Atisa pulling it out from his backpack, and Gaea looked at it puzzled. 'I remember the monk who asked if I wanted a picture of myself. And I showed him how to work the camera.' 'And did you find the Saka routes?'

'I did have an adventure almost like yours. When I was hiking in the mountains, I slipped and fell through a crack and found it led deep into a tunnel. I was actually very lost, and then really jumped out of my skin when someone emerged out of the darkness. He said he was from the tribe that was the keeper of these secret routes since time immemorial. You know, in the places I have been to – in the inaccessible grasslands of Mongolia or the mountain hideaways in Tibet, or even in the dry lost African villages or those deep in Guinea and in the Amazon – there are people who have their own sense of time. Theirs is a timeless world. And so I followed him as he led me out of the mountains, but I realized he was being cautious. "There is someone here, on these mountains," he told me, "who doesn't mean well." We were on an outcrop overlooking the river when we saw a man in a boat, and directly on the other side was a man with a catapult.' 'A catapult?'

'Yes, I had the same reaction, but the man with me, a warrior complete with his sword, bow and quiver full of arrows, said that the man with the catapult meant evil and that he had to do something to stop him. But he needed my help. There began a most fascinating duel across the river. The other man was aiming his deadly poisonous stones and the warrior deflected them all, but the man in the boat was clearly nervous. And in a particularly rough stretch of the water, the boat overturned, and we saw him hit his head against a rock and the man was also aiming his stones at him, and so one of us had to rush to his rescue.' 'And you sailed with him on the boat, and got him to safety,' said Atisa, who of course knew this bit of his mother's story.

'There was a temple, that I didn't know existed. But Dina...'

Atisa's heart leapt when he heard that name. So it was indeed Dina who had helped his mother as well. His mother went on, now totally concentrating on her story, 'Dina knew of this old temple of Shiva located deep in the jungle. That is where, he said, the man in the boat was headed. Dina also said that I must take him there while he battled this man who was bent on thwarting him at all costs. The priest was a different matter altogether. It was so exciting to get to that old temple. But the man needed help. He was already bleeding profusely and was delirious, so the only thing I could do as I went away to get help was to leave my transmitter for you. I hoped you would get the message. Of course, by the time I got out of the forests, I had lost all trace of what had happened. My maps didn't show anything, and I couldn't tell where the temple was for sure, and so I hoped you'd soon find out something with your special ways.'

She then showed him the routes that the Saka tribes had once used, routes that followed the old trading ways or the old lost rivers, and that was how she found herself back in Peshawar. She also told him about the frontier tribesman who showed her a secret way homeward. 'It took me a long time, but I was back home,' she ended happily. 'The longest route home is the shortest way home.' That evening, they had a quiet dinner, and not too long after, the storm rose outside to a howl. It thumped against the windows and rattled the old wooden doors. The trees creaked and bent, and on his sound catcher, he caught his father's reassuring voice on his transmitter. 'There's a storm here too, a real rough, cold one. We will have to delay our journey.'

But what his father said last mystified them all. 'Did you know there was an unexpectedly heavy snowmelt, and we had the herdsmen help us out. There were rivers of melted snow we had to ford and puddles deep enough to drown in, but the local herdsmen and their yaks were invaluable.' His father paused as if he knew what he would say next would have a dramatic impact on them. 'And guess what, a yak fell into the chasm, and when they retrieved him, they found a lost sack on him. And there were my lost cameras. They had just dropped into an abyss, and the snow had glued it back on to the yak.'

Atisa kept his thoughts to himself. Nurah's magical reappearances would be hard to explain anyway, but then he would be back again. He was certain of this. Next summer, for sure.